James Aiello

Forbidden Child.III.'Exposed'
Copyright 2015 by James Aiello
Productions, Inc.   This is a work of
fiction. All names and Characters are
either invented or used fictitiously. Any
resemblance to persons living or dead is
unintentional.   All rights reserved
under International and Pan-American
copyright conventions. No part of this
book may be reproduced, stored in a
retrieval system, or transmitted in any
form, electronic, mechanical, or other
means, now known or hereafter invented,
without written permission of author,
Author James Aiello
Cover Design: Graphic Art Designer, Tyler
J. Gillespie
ISBN- 978-0-692-59488-9
James Aiello Productions, Inc.
Vero Beach, FL32962CEO-
James Aiello
Jimgil99@yahoo.com

Table of Contents

Forbidden Child III Exposed

CHAPTER 1

It was 1:00am Pacific time when our flight left L.A. for Stewart Airport, and the whole world knew I was hopefully rushing home to Michael's arms. My emotions were raw and my energies were depleted from exposing my soul with such passion, it was all I could do just to get on the jet. Once seated, I placed my head on Jimmy's shoulder and stayed that way almost the entire flight home, without speaking for hours.

As I laid there with Jimmy gently stroking my head, I prayed, "Lord, please let him be home? Because if this doesn't do it, nothing will and you know how much I love him. Lord, I miss him so desperately, I'm honestly afraid I won't be able to live with the pain, if he's not. So please let him be home when I get there." But I found no solace nor comfort in that prayer; because I still feared Michael's seemingly unbendable Irish pride, could keep him from coming home to me. Then I decided I'd rather think of Michael being there, and the moment I did, my mind went wild with thoughts of passion.

As I envisioned my thoughts, I began to take notice of the movements of the aircraft which seemed to have been in a circling pattern for quite some time. So, I glanced at my watch which read 9:00am Eastern Standard time and I thought, "We should have landed by now?"

Curiosity took over as I sat up, reached to lift the window cover so I might glance out and just as I did, my new pilot, ex-lieutenant Todd Deyo opened the cabin door and said, "Excuse me Ms. Powers, but there has been a slight change in our landing plans."

"Is everything all right with the jet?" I asked in haste, as I quickly stood to my feet.

"The jet's fine Ma'am, it's the weather." he replied calmly. "Snow has been falling heavily over the region for hours now, and the tower at Stewart has rerouted all traffic to LaGuardia. So I'm afraid your arrival home will be delayed for quite some time."

"What?" I snapped with frustration. "I'm not waiting another day to get home! Are we over the airport right now?"

He was surprised by my angered response and I could tell as he cautiously answered, "Yes, Ma'am."

Studying his eyes I asked, "Todd, are you capable of landing this craft in a blizzard?" Without blinking he boldly replied, "Yes, Ma'am!"

I smiled at him confidently, "Good! Then let's go get you clearance."

Jimmy wore a stressed expression as he followed us into the cockpit and watched in silence, as I had Todd radio the tower. Once he had the chief traffic controller on the radio, Todd handed the extra headphone to me.

I clumsily put it on and said, "Hi, this is *Christina Powers*, with whom am I speaking?"

"This is Chief Controller Colonel Jeff Roberts, Ms. Powers. How may I help you?"

"Well Jeff, you could have a runway opened for us so we may land."

A polite yet firm voice replied, "I'm sorry Ms. Powers, but it's been deemed unsafe at this time. That is why your pilot has been ordered to proceed on a new coordinates."

To that I simply replied, "Jeff, forgive me, I'm

not normally this abrupt, but if you don't have a runway cleared for us in ten minutes, then I will see that the President hands me your career on a silver platter by this evening.   Capiche?"

Without a crack in his voice he replied, "Completely Ms. Powers, and you may inform your pilot to prepare for decent."

With a pleased tone I replied, "I thank you Colonel Roberts, and I will see that the President thanks you for me as well."

Todd smiled with amazement as he looked at me and said, "You might want to buckle up, this may be a slippery landing."

I studied his eyes once more as again I asked, "You can handle it, can't you?"

With a confident nod he answered, "Sure thing, Ma'am."

I chuckled and said, "Great, then we'll go make ourselves comfortable, and Todd, please call me Christina.   I prefer that to Ma'am, `cause I'm sure not as old as the word implies."   Then I nudged Jimmy whose mouth was on the floor and continued, "It will be fine, Jimmy. Now come on, let's go put our heads between our legs."

A nervous laugh began his come back, "Why, so we can kiss our asses' goodbye?"

"Don't panic I'm only kidding."   I replied with a chuckle.

He shook his head and said, "I know you want to get home, but don't you think you might be pushing it."

I smiled devilishly and said, "When have you known me not to push it, Jimmy?"   Then turning to my flight crew, I continued, "Now do a good job boy's, `cause I need to get home."

I reassured Jimmy with a confidant rustling of his

hair, as I buckled him in and said, "Lord willing we'll be down safely in ten minutes, so try not to worry."

"Thanks, that helps a lot!" He replied with a nervous look, "I should have stayed at the party with everyone else."

"What? And miss all this fun? That's not like you, Jimmy." I said with a smile as the jet began its descent. We were doing fine, even laughing as our ears popped on the descent, that was until the tires hit the pavement and Jimmy screamed, "Oh God!" as the jet immediately began a dramatic zig zagging slide down the runway. It wasn't two seconds before both of us were screaming out prayers as we were forcefully thrown from side to side in our seats for what seemed like an eternity, before finally slowing to a jerky stop. Realizing the danger was over I swallowed my heart, turned to Jimmy who was as white as a ghost, and started to laugh.

As soon as he caught his breath, he slapped my shoulder and shouted, "You think that was funny?"

"No, just ironic," I answered still laughing, "That little ride made me realize I love life too much to give up on it, even if Michael doesn't come home."

Once unbuckled, I went right into the cockpit to congratulate my crew on a job well done, and then said; "Now would someone please open that door so I can go home." The moment I saw the intensity of the blizzard we were walking into, I grabbed Jimmy's arm for strength and with a hopeless expression said, "He's not coming back, Jimmy."

"Yes he is, Christina." He answered with a big confident smile.

"No, he's not, Jimmy." I insisted with tears welling in my eyes, "Strangely, I've come to see the weather as the ultimate forecast of things to come in my life. And this storm is telling me to give it up girl, because you don't have a chance in hell of him coming home."

Jimmy squeezed my shoulder as we walked toward our warmed car and said, "Girlfriend, I know how much Michael loves you, and I know he's going to be there. So stop torturing yourself and I'll have us home in thirty minutes."

I kissed his cheek, "I hope you're right Jimmy, but the weather hasn't lied to me yet."

At that point, we reached the car and began to creep our way through the storm. As Jimmy drove, I pulled an envelope out of my purse, addressed it to Johnny, slipped his grandmother's ring in and had Jimmy stop at the first mailbox. I wrote nothing because there was nothing that needed to be said. Then, as I placed Michaels' ring back on my finger, I thought, "Weather you come home or not Michael, I will never take this ring off again."

Jimmy's thirty minutes turned into an hour and thirty minutes, before we pulled up to the house. As the large garage door began to open, my heart instantly pained. I turned to Jimmy with tears now streaming down my cheeks and cried, "His car is not here, Jimmy."

Jimmy looked at me before pulling into the garage, and said, "Well his car may not be here, but look who just stepped out onto the front porch." I turned quickly to see my beautiful man coming toward our car. My heart filled with excitement as I screamed, "Michael!" At that I jumped out of the car without my jacket and dashed through the snow toward him.

My sad tears instantly turned into joyful ones, as I leaped into his arms still screaming, "Michael! Michael! I love you! I love you, baby! I love you! Thank God, you're home!"

Forbidden Child III Exposed

"I love you too, Punkie!"   He shouted back as he lifted me into his arms.   Then gazing deep into my eyes he gently continued, "I love you more than life itself, and I'll never leave again, not even in death."   He kissed me with such passion that our souls were instantly whole again, and I knew he was home for good.

I clung to his neck as he held me like a babe in arms, and carried me toward the house.   When we reached the door he opened it, and charged up the staircase leaping three steps at a time.

He didn't slow his pace until we entered the bedroom, where he kissed me deeply as he laid me on the bed and softly whispered, "Don't move, Punkie." Then he proceeded to undress.

I watched in loving awe, as this god in the flesh tossed his clothing to the floor one piece at a time. Finally he dropped his last garment, and with the look I'd die for, returned to begin gently undressing me.   I couldn't help but lavish kisses all over his chest as he slipped the gown I still wore from my Grammy performance off my shoulders to expose the now hard nipples of my firm, bare, breasts.   As he leaned over to slide the gown from my hips I longingly and softly stroked the rest of his masculine body.

Slipping my last stocking off, he snuggled next to me and with a gentle air of dominance said, "Christina, you're my wife, and I'm proud to tell the world how much I love you.   All I ask is that you let me be your husband, not just someone who waits at home."

"Oh, Michael," I cried as I gazed into his eyes, "I love you, and I'm so sorry.   I was blind and foolish Michael, but I'm not anymore.   I want you to be my husband Michael, and I'm going to learn how to be your wife.   I promise."

Then sliding his leg over mine he said, "Before

we go any further, are you still on the pill?"

I lifted my head to kiss him passionately, then lovingly gazing at him I said, "No, Michael. I stopped taking them when we stopped making love."

He smiled peacefully and said, "I have a condom, let me get it."

I gently grabbed his hand and with loving conviction said, "Before you do, Michael, I need to say something. There is only one thing that could make my life totally complete right now, and that would be to conceive your child." Taking on an air of certainty I continued, "Please hear me, Michael? I have prayed and meditated nightly for weeks now, in an attempt to heal my body. So that if by the grace of God destiny brought us back together, then I would be able to carry our child. I know in my heart, Michael, that your seed will grow in me and I'll not only give birth, but I'll live through it as well." At that point I couldn't stop my tears as I continued, "Please, Michael plant your soul in mine so we may give birth to an angel."

He kissed me with joyful wonder and said, "I love you and I feel it too, Punkie! Deep in my soul, somehow I know you're healed! So with all my love I will give you my seed, and just like you sang, we'll watch it grow together." From that moment on we were swept up in a whirlwind of pure passion and unconditional love.

I was in heaven, as over and over we shared our love, and we didn't break our embrace until Jimmy came banging on the door shouting, "Hey guys! It's 7:00pm and you have to get up now it's urgent!"

I thought, 'Oh well, I'll figure it out tomorrow'. As I said, "What is it Jimmy?"

Carman fixed all your favorite 'aphrodisiacs' for dinner, and it will all be ready in twenty minutes. So would you guys like to be served in bed or would you prefer to join me in the dining room?"

I lifted my eyebrows as I looked at Michael and with a seductive smile said, "The menu sounds inviting, but I'll leave where we eat, up to you."

He returned my seductive smile with one of his own as he replied, "Let's go down and eat, then I can carry you back up again.   That was fun!"

I nibbled his nipple then said, "Au, now I can't wait to go down, just for the trip back up."

"Bang, Bang," came the second round of knocks as Jimmy shouted, "Do you guys hear me?"

"Yes." Michael replied, "We'll be right down, Jimmy."   Then we quickly showered and headed for the dining room.

As soon as we entered the dining room, Carman ran to us with tears in her eyes, hugged us both and said, "God has answered my prayers by bringing the two of you together again!   Now come sit, and let me serve you the first dinner of your new lives together."

I kissed her and said, "Thank you my sweet Carman that was beautiful."

Then Michael added, "Won't you and James share our meal with us tonight?"   Her face gleamed as she gracefully accepted.

We took our seats as Carman ran for James and our meal.

Jimmy entered the room with Pierre and a handful of newspapers, took his seat beside mine and with an excited tone said, "You guys are not going to believe today's headlines.   Listen to this one, **'Only Christina Powers could pull off the controversial substitution of a Grammy performance and be given a standing ovation.'** Or this one, **'Christina Powers' daring Grammy performance last evening,**

establishes her as the icon of the twenty first century, as millions of worldwide viewers immediately swamped their local radio stations with requests for the song the callers themselves called, 'Michael My Love'.' Can you believe this response from your fans?" Jimmy continued, "It's phenomenal!"

Michael and I were both shocked as headline after headline repeated the same sentiments.

After reading the articles I looked at Michael with a concerned expression and said, "We need to really talk Michael, because this is scaring me."

He leaned over to kiss me, "I'm here now Punkie, and you don't have to worry about anything tonight, except me.   We'll deal with the world tomorrow."

I was truly comforted by his words when I returned his kiss and said, "You're right Michael, because there's one thing I've learned, everything else is secondary to us."

Pierre now sitting next to Jimmy jumped in, "Christina, I've never seen anything like it.   I watched the Grammys in our main auditorium with about 200 other employees and the entire place was stunned when you started singing a different song, but one minute into it they were all crying and loved it.   You are truly loved by so many people Christina and I love you too my friend."

"Thank you Pierre that was sweet."   I leaned over kissed his check then Jimmy's, "and it's good to see you two together again.   I'm so happy for you both."

Just then, Carman entered the dining room with a feast fit for two kings. When our meal was complete Michael did exactly as he promised, swept me off my feet and carried me back to our boudoir, where we continued exactly where we left off.

It was 4:00am when I slipped out of Michael's

Forbidden Child III Exposed

sleepy embrace, and tiptoed through the dimly lit bedroom to the master bath. When I returned, Michael was sitting on the edge of the bed, and as I approached he beckoned me to sit next to him. I submissively took my place beside him and he gently drew me into his embrace. I snuggled to his chest as he tenderly said, "I love you Christina, and it's now my turn to say I'm sorry. I know I wasn't there when you needed me either, I guess I was afraid to hear what you had to say. So Punkie, if you're up to telling me what happened in Saudi Arabia, I'm up to listening."

I held him tightly as the frightening; bizarre memories of that trip and the one that followed came flashing back. It was at that moment I finally felt safe enough to show the fear I truly felt, and I began to weep as my body trembled from the images exploding in my mind. I told him about Mohammed and how he nearly took me life three times. First he tried to throw me off a roof top, then he tried to blow me up in a helicopter, and the last time I saw him he tried to kill me by hand. I had to hold a sword to this throat to stop him. It happened in Iraq when I went to free the hostages. He led me into a massive library, where he proceeded to go through a large old book of Islamic Prophecies. Finding what he was looking for, he said, "You read Arabic, read it for yourself."

I took the book and glancing to where he was pointing began to read, "**At the time of the alignment of all celestial bodies within your solar system, the king's daughter shall rise to power and she shall be known to the world as the 'Angel of Peace'. This one is the mother of the Messiah, who is the daughter of the king and the descendants of Abraham. Her power is in her tongue of many languages, and she alone shall marry the true heir to the throne of David**

and bear him his first male child. The child she brings forth in the wilderness shall be the pure descendant of Adam's seed, and he represents the true returning of the Prince of Peace. He alone will finally usher in the Heavenly Millennium of paradise on earth foretold by the prophets."

As I finished, I closed the book and said, "I'm not usually this bad with puzzles, but I still don't get the connection."

Looking at me as if I were an imbecile he said, "You, Christina, are that woman. The one the world calls the 'Angel of Peace', and I am the rightful heir to the throne of David."

I shook my head in total disbelief and said, "You really put all this together just from a newspaper article which called me the 'Angel of Peace?'"

Taking the book from my hands, he placed it on the shelf. He turned back toward me, and taking me in his arms, he lovingly said, "That is not the only reason my love, you are rising to power in the world whether you realize it or not. The alinement of the planets spoken of in this prophecy will take place in May of the year 2000, and you are also fluent in many languages. I know everything there is to know about you. I have always known in my heart, you would one day be my bride and bear me my son. Together through peace, we shall conquer the world and give it to our son, who will lead all peoples into a millennium of peace on earth."

I had to push hard to get out of his loving embrace as I said, "Please, Mohammed, not so close, I like my space. I have got to say for someone who supposedly knows so much about me, then how come you overlooked the fact I can no longer bear children. Doesn't that put a damper on your theories as to whom you think I am?"

Forbidden Child III Exposed

He was slowly coming closer to me with a very hungry look on his face as he said, "I know about your injury. If you let me, I will teach you how to heal your wounds from within. You can tap into the divine power, which is yours, and I know how it's done. Then, you will be able to bear our child. The secrets of God's power are at your disposal Christina, it lies within."

He was still slowly continuing to walk toward me as I backed away. Putting my hands up to slow his descent upon me and thinking quick I said, "You're not listening Mohammed, I just told you I can no longer bear children."

I could see in his eyes he was beginning to become upset with my resistance when he said, "You're the one not listening! You already have the power to heal yourself."

As my back reached the wall I said, "Well, I hope I can grow back a uterus, because that's what it's going to take."

His face became as white as a ghost. He took a deep breath, while hovering over me shouting, "What are you talking about!?"

That was the moment I knew I was heading for trouble and I thought, 'Lord Jesus, please help me out of this one!' As I said, "I nearly lost my life last year in an attempt to have a child. While I was unconscious, the doctors had to perform a hysterectomy on me in order to save my life."

His eyes became red with anger. With one hand, he took my left shoulder and flung me with such force, I went flying into a book shelf sending the books toppling on top of my head. Lying under a pile of books I heard him yelling, "This can't be! I thought you were the one!"

As I looked up from under the books, I could see

he was coming to give me some more, so just as he reached down to grab me, I pushed up with my legs knocking him into another book shelf. I scrambled to my feet, went running for the door and of course it was locked. I turned quickly to see where he was, and he was coming right for me. I screamed out with all my might, "Stop this, Mohammed! This is *madness*! Help! Someone help!"

Looking around quickly, I spotted two swords mounted on the wall. I grabbed for the sword which hung on the wall about four feet from me. When I had it, I swung around as fast as lightening just in time to hold its sharp point right at his throat. He stopped dead in his tracks and as I backed him into a book shelf I shouted, "Get it together or I won't hesitate to use this! I'll do it right now you crazy bastard!"

Suddenly, Lussein with twenty guards, burst into the room and Lussein shouted, "Mohammed, if we take her life now we will be destroying all our future plans. Calm down my brother and know one day, you will have your revenge on this temptress from the depths of hell. Besides, I told you she was not the one, now leave her alone and let her go back to her demon possessed nation where trash like her belong."

The thought of Lussein's prediction at that moment, nearly made me cut Mohammed's head off right on the spot. It took all my self-control not to lunge forward and plunge the blade right through him, but I thought, 'It's not worth it Christina, he's just an evil man.'

Within moments Mohammed calmed himself down and with his angelic voice said, "I'm sorry if I hurt you, but your news was devastating and it made me upset."

Still holding the sword to Mohammed's neck I

looked toward Lussein and said, "You told the President you would release the hostages to me, now I'm tired of fooling around here, so please release them and let us leave at once."

With a deadly serious look in his eyes, he said, "If you give your word you will not tell anyone that Mohammed was here, you may leave now."

I smiled and reassuringly said, "You've got a deal!"

He clapped his hands, turned to his guards and shouted, "Take Ms. Powers to the airport immediately."

"Wait just a minute," I demanded. "I'm not going anywhere without the hostages."

Lussein walked right up to my face while I still held the sword and said, "You really are a gutsy broad."

Without blinking once I replied, "Thank you. I'll take that as a compliment, now please bring out the hostages."

He smiled and his smile seemed to hold a slightly detectable glimmer of admiration as he said, "It's all right to go with the guards Christina, the hostages are already boarded on your jet and waiting for you."

Looking into his eyes, I knew he was telling the truth; so, I thanked him as I handed him the sword. Confidently, I proceeded to walk out of that room holding my head held high with an air about me, as if I had total control over this insane situation and not thinking of losing my composure the entire time. But inside, I was a frightened little girl. Then I started to cry again

Michael rocked me in his strong comforting arms until I cried it all out. Hee listened intently as I told him the whole nightmarish ordeal.

He looked baffled by the time I finished speaking then said, "My God, I could shoot myself for not being there for you."

"Don't say that, Michael, you're here now and that's what counts."

He kissed me gently, "What do you think it all means?"

I hid nothing of myself as I gazed into his eyes and said, "I'm not sure, honey! But something tells me I'll be hearing from Mohammed Fehd again, and that thought leaves me spooked."

"Don't be." Michael said angrily, "Because I'll kill anyone who tries to harm you!"

I hugged him again, "I love you Michael, and believe it or not, I know I'll always be safe with you beside me."

Then gazing into the open thoughts on his face, I could see there was one more thing that needed to be settled. So I tenderly took his hand in mine and said, "Michael, baby, I don't want to keep anything from you ever again. So if you will allow me, I'd like to tell you about my past relationship with John Everett."

He looked lovingly at me as he said, "Just for the record please answer two things for me, then I'll never mention it again. Did you sleep with him since we've been together, and do you still have feelings for him?"

I kissed his cheek as I proudly said, "The answer is no baby, to both your questions." Squeezing his arm as I continued, "Michael, I've only loved and longed for you since our first kiss."

He sighed then smiled as he said, "I was pretty sure of the answers, but it's sure good to you hear them from you." He kissed me passionately, then gently rubbing my belly added, "By the grace of God, we have the union of our love growing inside of you right now Punkie, and I know we're going to have our family." He took on the most sincere expression I'd ever seen from anyone as he continued, "Christina, I want to take you and our child away from here. I want us to have a normal life without all the craziness. I guess what I'm asking is for you to give it all up for me." As tears welled in his eyes, "Can you do that? Can you give it all up for a family life with me?"

"Yes," I cried as I wrapped my arms around his neck. "Oh Michael, my love, I would put a match to it all and watch it burn, if it brought our souls together for all eternity."

His face lit up with joy as he said, "Then let's start by leaving Jimmy in charge for a year or so this time, while we go start our family. We could tell him at breakfast and be on our way by lunch."

I was surprised by his spontaneity, so I chuckled as I said, "Michael, if you want to leave now and never come back, then I'm ready. Because I'll follow you to heaven or hell, and all you have to do is lead."

"Oh Baby, I love you! You just made me the happiest man on earth." He said these words as he laid me back onto the pillows, and once more began to fill me with his essence. The love we felt as we made love after the conversation of that morning had a divine power to it that was beyond words.

Later that morning over breakfast, Michael informed a now stunned Jimmy of our immediate plans to leave, then said, "Jimmy, I'm not sure how long we're going to be gone or where we'll even end up, but I do know it's our turn to find a life. So we're just leaving it all in your hands until we know for sure what we're doing."

Jimmy looked sad as he replied, "I understand guys, and I'll take care of everything, because I know this is the best thing for both of you." He started to cry, "It's just that I'm going to miss you guys. You're my family and we've been apart for so long already."

I hugged him and said, "Jimmy, we're not leaving you, just the madness of this lifestyle. You will always be my brother and welcomed into our home wherever we live."

"That's right!" Michael added, "And like I said Jimmy, it's not forever and we'll let you know what's going on with us when we know."

Still sad, but at least smiling he murmured, "I love you guys, and I hope you find the happiness you both deserve. All I ask is that you don't forget me."

I laughed, "Forget about you. That's impossible, Jimmy."

We all started to laugh, then Michael stood up and said, "Now that that's settled, I'll go make some travel arrangements."

"So you do know where you're going." Jimmy interrupted. "Well at least tell me where you're headed?"

Michael smiled mischievously as he said, "Don't worry about where we're going right now Jimmy, I want to keep it a surprise for my wife." He kissed me and added, "I'll be back in a few minutes then we'll get out of here."

"Already," I said with a surprised tone. "Shouldn't we pack some things first?"

He smiled again and said, "Carman already packed for us and James is putting the suitcases in the trunk of the car right now. I've also called our head of security Frank Rossi and he is working on getting us out of here without the press finding out."

I kissed him back and said, "You're not wasting any time are you?"

Jimmy interrupted again, but this time his voice was panicked, "Wait, what about the song? Michael, we have millions of fans wanting to buy that song, you can't take Christina away without recording it first."

"I didn't know it wasn't recorded." Michael answered, then turning to me with a look of frustration, "Christina, if we stay for that we may never get out of here."

I thought for a minute then said, "I got it! Jimmy, have a recording and a video cut from the tape of the Grammy performance to release to the public as a single. Title it, 'Michael My Love.' Then feature it as the lead cut on a greatest hits soundtrack. Just don't include any of the cuts from the 'Halloween in Hell' soundtrack."

"That's a great idea." Jimmy said with a big smile, "I could have it ready in no time that way." Then with the flick of that wrist he added, "Just like I've always said, you are a 'fucking genius', girlfriend!"

Michael was still standing next to me when he said, "I think I'll go make that call before something else comes up."

And just as he said those words, Carman entered the dining room with the cordless phone and said, "Excuse me Christina, but the President is on the phone for you."

"What now!" Michael said with disgust.

I took his hand reassuringly, "Don't panic Michael, let's just see what he wants." I took the phone from Carman and said, "Hi George, how are you?"

"I'm great now that Kuwait is liberated and the ground war is over. But how are you? Did Michael come home?"

I chuckled with a sense of relief, "Yes, he did George, and it's sweet of you to call and ask."

"Well, you only happen to be the second hottest story in the headlines, and the last report I heard, neither one of you showed up for the divorce proceedings. And since I was calling anyway, I thought I might be one of the first to find out for sure."   At that, his voice took on a tone of sincerity as he continued, "You're a good friend Christina, and Barbara and I are very pleased for the both of you."

I felt honored hearing words of friendship coming from our nation's leader, so I gracefully replied, "I thank you again, George.   It means a great deal to me to be considered your friend. Now I don't mean to rush you, but let's get to the other reason for your call, because Michael and I were just on our way out the door as you rang."

He chuckled, "We're not ones to waste time beating around the 'bush' are we?"

"You got that right!"   I laughed, as Michael rushed me with his hand gestures.

"Now for the other reason for my call; I would like to bestow the Distinguished Citizens Award upon you, during tomorrow night's Presidential address to Congress and the nation. I also plan to take this occasion to announce my bid for reelection. I hope to have you standing beside me at the news conference to follow, so you may throw your full support behind my reelection bid at the same time."

"I'm more than honored George," I said with surprise.   "But I'm not sure I can make it. Let me have you speak with Michael, he's handling my schedule now."   I handed the phone to Michael who was motioning, 'no, no,' with his hands as I whispered, "You have to talk to him Michael, because I don't know what to say."

Michael took the phone with apprehension, "Hello Mr. President, how can we help you?"

CHAPTER 2

The next thing I knew, we were on our way to Washington for dinner with the President and First Lady for that very evening.

To our surprise that evening's dinner included not only the President and First Lady, but also every Republican politician and foreign dignitary in Washington. Only Michael and I were not aware of this fact until we entered the dining hall, and the entire dinner party rose to their feet applauding. Then, as we were led to the President's table, we were greeted by everyone we passed with warm smiles, handshakes, and words of admiration.

This only intensified when we reached the President who raised his glass to us and said, "Dear Friends, I would like to make a toast tonight to a woman, who in her young life span has gone from being called the 'queen of bleeding heart liberals' to the 'angel of peace'." Smiling he continued, "Well now it's my turn to coin a phrase at your expense Christina, only this time I bestow it upon Michael as well. Here's to 'the most passionate couple on earth'. Bravo Michael and Christina!"

We drank to the toast and were cheered again, "Bravo Michael and Christina!"

After dinner, we were formally invited by the majority of the foreign diplomats whose citizens I helped release from Iraq, on behalf of their nation's leaders to visit their countries.

Michael and I were overwhelmed by the reception we received that night, and it didn't end there. For the next evening, after the President's address we were given another standing ovation. Only this time, it was by all of Congress broadcasted on national TV, when with Michael beside me, I received the Distinguished Citizens Award for my contributions in freeing the multinational group of Iraqi hostages. At the informal news conference/celebration which followed, the President once again grandstanded Michael and me, as he announced his bid for reelection.

Immediately after his announcement he turned the podium over to Michael and me both by saying, "Barbara and I have invited our dear friends, Michael and Christina Powers Gillespie, to share their thoughts with us this evening. So now I'd like to turn all attention over to the Gillespie's."

Everyone applauded as I moved to the mike still holding Michael's hand and said, "Good evening friends. And it truly has been a good evening, especially for Michael and me. That's why we'd like to say a special thank you to the people of this great nation of ours for your love and support. We'd also like to thank the President and First Lady for giving us this glorious evening. Now I'd like to come to the other reason I'm standing here tonight and that is to throw my full political support behind the President's bid for reelection. Believe me; I don't take this endorsement lightly either. I have come to this decision from having worked side-by-side with the President, and seeing first-hand how he deals with our country and world issues. I believe he has proven himself to be a great leader, and that is why I am able to say, George you have earned my vote." With that I received a standing ovation.

That evening, we were catapulted as a couple into the political spotlight by the arms of the entire Republican Party as they embraced us whole heartedly. Let me tell you, 'the smellier stuff' was flowing so thick that night, that even my ex-husband, Senator Lee Bradford invited Michael and me to a party in the President's honor, at the Republican Party's New York Headquarters in Manhattan.

Michael took all this attention quite well, that was until the President came to us privately and said, "Michael, I'd like to have you and Christina join me at one more campaign banquet tomorrow evening."

Michael didn't even look at me when he said, "I'm very sorry Mr. President, but Christina and I are leaving for our second honeymoon right at this very moment, so I'm afraid we can't make it to any more gatherings."

George looked at me with a surprised expression and said, "But Christina, I was counting on your support. That's why I've already made a public announcement that the two of you would be accompanying me to tomorrow night's banquet."

I smiled mischievously, "Good try George, but I'm sorry you took the liberty to do that without discussing it with us first. Like Michael said, we were just leaving, so I'm afraid you're going to have to make our apologies for us." I kissed his stunned cheek, hugged the First Lady, took Michael's hand and said our goodbyes as we swiftly made our way through the crowd.

It wasn't until we were sitting comfortably, snuggled in each other's arms and in the air that I said, "So where are you taking me anyway?"

He smiled mischievously and answered, "First

tell me, how long it will be before we know for sure if you're pregnant?"

"Probably another twelve days. Why?" I asked with interest. "What does that have to do with where you take me on our second honeymoon?"

"It's only because I don't want you to over-do it, that's all."

"Okay smarty, but you still haven't answered my question, where are we going?"

"Well I wanted it to be a surprise, but I guess I can tell you now. It was the strangest thing. The minute we decided to try and have a baby again something told me to prepare a family tree for our child. So I thought what better way than to go back to the countries of our forefathers to make one. That's why I've planned two weeks in Ireland to find my side of the tree, and another two weeks in Italy to find your side of the tree." Smiling with excitement he added, "So what do you think?"

I was speechless realizing for the first time that I have never told anyone, not even Michael who my true parents were. His smile turned into a frown as he said, "Gee! I thought it was a good idea."

I still said nothing, not knowing how to answer him until with a very concerned look he said, "Christina, what is it? You look as though you've seen a ghost."

Gazing up into his eyes with intensity I said, "I have Michael, and it's a ghost from my past."

With a wondering look he asked, "I don't understand what you're saying, what ghost from your past?"

I slipped out of his arms so I could sit up and look directly into his eyes as I said, "Michael honey, do you remember I told you that I was keeping no more secrets from you?"

His expression went from wondering to concern as he calmly said, "Yes."

"There is one more thing about myself that I have never repeated to a soul since the moment I heard it. I guess it's because I never really wanted to face it myself, so how could I talk about it?"

Michael knew I was struggling when he took my hand and said, "Punkie, I will love you no matter what ghosts may haunt you. I thought you realized that by now?"

I smiled and said, "Yes Michael, I do realize that, and I know there's nothing that we can't conquer together." Kissing his cheek I continued, "That's why finally, I know I have the courage to face what I'm about to tell you." At that, I proceeded to tell him everything Frank Salerno said to me that awful day so long ago. Then I told him that Barbara gave me my birth certificate and a letter from my true mother after Frank's death.

Michael was overwhelmed by my revelation and with a look of wonder the first thing he said was, "Oh my God, you are the daughter of a king."

"What?" I said with nervous surprise. "Why would you say that?"

He shook his head with concern, "The first thing that came to my mind was that nut Mohammed's, prophecy."

Looking at him intensely I asked, "What do you think it means, Michael?"

"I don't know Babe, but something tells me the answer lies somewhere in Ireland."

"Ireland! Why there?" I asked with a baffled expression.

"Don't you see this changes things." He said with wide eyes, "We've known I've had a full-blooded Irish heritage all along, and now we know your father

26

Forbidden Child III Exposed

was also Irish. So all we need to do is discover your mother's true bloodline and I think we'll find our answer."

I shook my head with a confused look, "I think you lost me. What does my mother's heritage have to do with Mohammed's prophecy?"

"I don't know, but something tells me we'll find out when we know more about your true mother's bloodline."

CHAPTER 3

Our two weeks in Ireland turned out to be quite interesting as we discovered many similar thing's about our forefathers. For example, on Michael's side the Gillespie's and the Carr's were both from the same village as the Kenney's on my father's side were. But the most interesting of all, was our discovery that my mother's biological father could have been a man named John O'Hara, who's family also happened to originate from the same Irish town and if that were true, then I would also have an Irish heritage.

The afternoon we made this discovery we were in the hall of records in Dublin, and I turned to Michael with a bewildered expression and asked, "Michael, what do you think it all means?"

He smiled gently, "I think it means that Mohammed was wrong, it's not his child in the prophecy, it's ours."

I looked at him strangely, "I still don't get it. What does the fact that I'm Irish and not Italian have to do with Mohammed's prophecy? I'd have to be Jewish to fit his prophecy." Then I laughed out loud, "You can't think the Irish race could be the true lost tribe of Israel, do you?"

He answered with a very serious tone, "I think anything is possible. Furthermore I think God is telling us that it is our baby who is destined for great things."

Forbidden Child III Exposed

I kissed him, smiled and said, "I am sure of that, Michael, without a prophecy. What I'm not sure of, is weather I'm even pregnant or not yet."

He laughed, hugged me and replied, "Well why don't we go back to the motel and use that test kit you bought, so we can finally find out."

I kissed him again and with a sexy smile said, "Let's go for it big boy." And off we headed for the motel.

I came out of the bath holding a test strip in two fingers, and as I reached an anxious Michael I said, "Keep your fingers crossed, honey."

"How does it work?" He asked intently.

"We wait two minutes and if it turns red then it's a go, but if it turns blue then we keep trying."

We were breathless as the color began to take on a greenish tint, then to our dismay it turned utterly blue, and as soon as it did, Michael whined with disappointment, "Oh no!"

I threw the strip away, hugged him, and said, "It's all right, honey. It will turn red, I know it will." Then I slipped my hand into his pants, "And we'll just keep trying until it does."

He kissed me, swept me off my feet and as he headed for the bedroom he said, "You can bet your sweet buns on that, Punkie!" When we reached the bedroom he placed my feet on the floor as his lips engulfed mine. He released his hold of me and gently commanded, "Dance for your Daddy and take those clothes off."

I immediately preformed for him the way only I could and the last garment stripped was his bikini brief. I found myself on my knees in front of the man I loved and I began to devourer him with every drop of my passion. In perfect rhythm I lusted and longed for each thrust he gave me. As I looked up into his eyes and he

Forbidden Child III Exposed

said, "I love seeing you in that position baby. You're so beautiful Christina….Oh yea…make love to your Daddy baby girl."

We were nearly to the point of ecstasy when he stopped our dance and gently lifted me from on my knees and placed me on the bed.

"Oh baby." I moaned as he began to gently caress my breast.   I felt so much love for him that I surrendered totally to his slightest touch and as his lips surrounded my engorged nipple my body became electrified. "Take me Daddy, I'm yours." was all I could say as we became one.   And for the next three hours he seduced me with his every movement.

It was 9:00pm when we decided to wash and go for dinner, and as we strolled hand in hand, through the historical streets of 'Old Dublin' I said, "Now that we have our family trees, what would you like to do next, Michael?"

He put his arm around my shoulder and said, "I've been thinking about that.   And I think that since we're in Europe anyway, we should try to visit as many of the nations whose leaders have invited us.   They all want to thank you formally for helping free their citizens and I think it's only right that we go.   At least until you've conceived; and we can check that every couple of days.   This way, we still get to be together and we can enjoy Europe at the same time.   What do you think?"

I kissed him with excitement and said, "I think it sounds great, baby! I've wanted us to be able to go away like this forever."   The next morning we were making arrangements to visit the heads of state throughout Europe beginning with England.

We arrived in London on March 17th, 1991, and we were treated like royalty, even by members of the royal family themselves, including the Queen.   She made me an Honorary British Citizen for my gallant efforts in obtaining the freedom of thirty six British citizens. It was incredible, everywhere we went the people of England greeted us with cheers as they held signs which read, **"We love you Christina and Michael!"** And the headlines read, **"America's first couple; 'Christina and Michael' are welcomed with opened arms by all of Britain."**

We stayed two weeks in England then it was off to France for two weeks. Since I still hadn't conceived, we decided to take our traveling to Italy. From there it was off to Spain, Greece, Germany, Switzerland, Russia, Romania, India, China, South Korea, Japan and in September we ended up in Australia. And everywhere we went the reaction to us as a couple was the same, warm and loving. It seemed that as the fame of 'Michael My Love' spread, so did the mystique of our relationship. It was as if the whole world decided to place us as a magical couple on top of an international pedestal to be admired and idolized. The treatment we received was so overwhelming and enticing that we became perfect at playing the part of America's royal couple.

We arrived in Australia on September 7th, at 9:00pm, to a hero's welcome at the airport. We were taken by an official government escort to our hotel in beautiful downtown Sydney. As we checked in, Michael grabbed the usual pile of telegrams waiting for us at the front desk and we headed to our suite. After settling in I began to open the telegrams.

With the first one I opened, I turned to Michael and with a nervous tone said, "Oh no Michael, it's from him."

"From whom?" He asked as he walked toward me.

Forbidden Child III Exposed

"Prince Mohammed Fehd," I answered. "Listen to this, '**Dear Christina, I see you have successfully salvaged your pitiful marriage. What a shame to waste such energy and passion on a common peasant, when you could have had a god. At least your foolish actions have proven to me that you are definitely not the woman I thought you were. Once my eyes were opened, I was finally able to find my true queen. That's why I took as my bride the daughter of King Sada of Syria, Princess Jasmine on August 25th of this year. I know she will bear the child I foolishly hoped would be ours, but I also know she will never fill my heart with the passion I felt just from kissing your hand. So regretfully, I must now say goodbye to my dream of you Christina, for it's time to fulfill my destiny. I also know I will always carry the pain of an unquenched flame within my soul for you my love. Forever, Prince Mohammed Fehd.**"

"Can you believe this," I said shaking my head?

"Well at least it sounds like we won't be hearing from him again."

I chuckled and said, "I hope she gives him three hundred kids to rule the world; that ought to keep them busy for a while."   At that we laughed it off.

But what transpired the following morning took the laughter away. It was 10:00am September 8th, when we took our seats with Australia's Prime Minister Mark Amentia, to view the extravagant parade which was held in honor of our visit. That morning Sidney was alive with the sounds of marching bands and shouts of admiration and love, for their adored visitors, 'Christina and Michael'.

As I sat there watching thousands of people cheering as they passed by, 'suddenly' it hit me and my eyes were opened as if for the first time since we left Ireland. The awakening frightened me as I realized Michael and I were unconsciously becoming sanctimonious, as both of us were being sucked into the vacuous powers of international idolatry. And the speed at which we were catapulting toward our world image of some god like couple, was so phenomenal that I thought, 'Oh my God! We're becoming just like Mohammed; thriving on the admiration of the masses and the power that comes with it, instead of thriving on helping the masses and the satisfaction that comes from it.'

At that moment, with that thought, I caught sight of an old gray haired woman wearing shredded rags. I watched as she began to slowly make her way across the street, right through the marching bands toward us. As she came closer, I could see pain in her eyes with every step she took and my heart went out to her. She walked right past the Prime Minister's security guards and began to climb up the twenty or so steps toward where we were seated. I was surprised no one stopped her, but I said nothing because I couldn't take my eyes off this pitiful woman.

I just sat there staring and when she reached me, she took my hand in her withered one, looked straight into my eyes and with a weakened voice said, "Christina my child, there appeared a great wonder in heaven, a woman clothed with the sun and the moon. And under her feet and upon her head a crown of twelve stars. And she-being with child cried, travailing in birth and pained to be delivered. And there appeared another wonder in heaven and behold a great red dragon, having seven heads and ten horns and seven crowns upon his heads. And his tail drew the third part of the stars of heaven and he did cast them to the earth."

Forbidden Child III Exposed

Then she pointed one shaky finger at me as she continued, "And then the dragon stood before the woman who was ready to be delivered, to devour her child as soon as it was born. And she brought forth a man child, who was to rule all nations with a rod of iron and her child was caught up unto God and to his throne. And the woman fled into the 'mountains', where she hath a place prepared of God that they should feed her there a thousand two hundred and threescore days, at which time war shall breakout in heaven and it shall spill over onto earth. But do not fear for God is with you my child."

With that she let go of my hand and as I began to shake, the medallion I found so many years ago with Tony, began to burn my skin. At that split second I quickly pulled the medallion from my chest, as I nervously turned to Michael, grabbed his hand and said, "Michael, listen to this woman!" I turned back and my heart froze with fear for she was gone. I looked at Michael again only this time I was as white as a ghost and I said, "Michael, something's wrong! Please get me out of here!"

Instantly, without even asking me what was wrong, he made our excuses and had us swiftly escorted back to our hotel. As soon as we entered the room Michael closed the door behind us and said, "What is it, Punkie?"

I clung to his chest for strength and answered, "Michael, something is telling me that our rise in popularity is a trap to keep us from having a child. And as long as we continue to stay on this course, I will never conceive our child." Then I looked into his eyes with fear in mine and added, "Michael, did you see that old lady?"

"What old lady?" He answered with a confused

look.

A cold chill shot up my spine, "The one who was talking to me right in front of you."

He held me tight as he answered, "No Punkie, I didn't see or hear anyone."

I pulled out of his arms and proceeded to tell him what she said to me, and when I finished I said, "Honey, I don't know what's going on here, but I know I'd feel much better if we were home."

He had a curious look on his face when he said, "I think you're right we should go home. Only I think home should be our Catskill 'Mountain' House."

I hugged him and with a sigh of relief said, "Oh Michael, I love you!   I feel a sense of peace already, just knowing where we're going."

He kissed me lovingly and excitedly said, "So do I, Punkie! Why don't we make our excuses and leave now?"

"Could we, Michael?"   I asked eagerly.

"Sure we could."

"Great, then I'm going to go to speak with Frank Rossi our security chief, I'll be right back." I went right to Frank's makeshift office and when I walked in I said, "Frank, I want to speak with you in private. Michael and I want to go back home. Frank, I would like to ask you to arrange it so that we can enter the country without anyone finding out.   Do you think you can arrange it?"

This beautifully handsome six foot tall man looked at me through eyes of pure adoration as he said, "Christina, I don't just consider you my employer, I respect you immensely and I consider you one of my best friends. I would do anything for you my friend. And I can assure you that no one will know you're back in the states."

I hugged him, "Thank you, how soon do you

think we can get home?"

He smiled reassuringly, "You start packing and I'll start calling."   And not two hours later **we were on our way home.**

CHAPTER 4

In an attempt to avoid the fanfare we decided not to tell anyone, except Jimmy and the proper authorities that we were returning home. Believe it or not at 1:00am on September 9th, 1991, we entered the country without one reporter finding out, thanks to my security chief Frank Rossi. Inconspicuously, we made our way through the airport and headed straight for our waiting car. Like two emotionally exhausted and mentally bewildered children, we drove off into the darkness hoping to find a place to hide and reflect. As we drove up the winding path of 23A to Tannersville and our mountain top hideaway, I took Michael's hand and said, "Michael, look at how beautifully the stars are shining tonight."

He brought my hand to his lips, kissed it and said, "Whoa, the sky really is bright! I can't remember seeing a night this bright since I was a child growing up on this mountain." Glancing my way with a relieved smile he continued, "And let me tell you Punkie, it sure feels good to be on familiar ground again. How about you? Are you feeling any better?"

I smiled my reply, "I feel like the weight of the world has been lifted off my shoulders, just from knowing we'll soon be home." In a serious tone I added, "But honey, I still can't get that old woman out of my mind, and for the life of me I can't figure it out.

Forbidden Child III Exposed

Then I thought, if it really was a message of some kind, then why can't I understand it?"

"I've been thinking a lot about what she said." Michael replied softly. "Now I'm not sure, but I think I may have read something similar to her words in the Bible. When I get a chance I'll take a look and see if I can find it. But as for making sense of it, maybe she was telling you the world's attention was like a beast. After all, she did come just as you realized we were being caught up by all the glorified notoriety, didn't she? So maybe she was saying this beast was somehow keeping us from having a child."

With a mysterious tone I said, "That's funny! I thought the same thing, but I dismissed it thinking it couldn't be that simple."

Just then we pulled into the driveway of Michael's family house and joyfully he said, "We're finally home, Punkie!" With that, we climbed out of the car and headed hand-in-hand toward the house.

Halfway up the walk I stopped, wrapped my arms around his neck and said, "I love you, Michael." Then I kissed him and added, "Maybe now that we're home we'll be able to start our family."

He returned my kiss passionately, "I don't think we should waste one more minute getting started either."

I laughed, then with a seductive smile shouted, "Last one on the porch has to undress the other." Then I took off running as I continued shouting, "With no hands!"

He charged after me and leaped into the lead just as we reached the porch. I jumped on his back shouting, "No fair! You have longer legs then I do."

I was still on his back laughing and nipping at his ear as he tried to open the door while twisting his head and saying, "I'm going to get you if you don't stop."

Forbidden Child III Exposed

We entered that lonely, quiet mountain house with love, laughter, and renewed anticipation for our future family. The house was chilly when we raced in, so I quickly started making hot cocoa, while Michael built a fire in the bedroom fireplace. I had two buttered English Muffins to accompany our cocoa when I entered the bedroom. But as soon as I saw Michael through the fire-lit room, lying on the bed with nothing on, I knew we weren't about to eat English Muffins. So, I placed the tray on the night stand then slowly moved between the bed and the fireplace where I very seductively began to undress for my man. When there was nothing left to remove, Michael reached his hand out to mine. As I took hold of his hand, he pulled me into the bed and began to tickle me till I was laughing so hard, I was begging him to stop. When he did stop, he placed my hand on his now firm muscle and with a sexy smile said, "It's all yours Punkie, tonight and every night for as long as you can get it up."

"Wow, all mine," I replied with a big grin. Then figuring it was now my turn I added, "Good, then you won't mind if I break it off." I began to playfully squeeze his pride and joy as I laughed, "Tickle me will you, I know how to get even."

"Stop, Christina stop," he pleaded from between his laughter.

I let go and said, "Oh poor, baby! Do you need me to kiss it and make it all better?"

"I couldn't think of anything I'd like more." He replied with a sweet grin.

We found ourselves feeling so comfortable and free from being home, we spent the rest of that wonderfully romantic night, lovingly and playfully becoming one. Our love was so deep and peaceful that we both knew we were moving mountains, and two

Forbidden Child III Exposed

weeks to the date, the test strip I held confirmed I was pregnant. We looked at each other with our hearts in our eyes as we watched the thin strip quickly turn red. With tears streaming down our faces, we leaped into each other's arms screaming. I grabbed his hand and shouted, "Come with me!" I pulled him out the back door and began running into the sunshine toward the clearing in the back yard, which gazed out over the valley and the river below. When we reached it, I shouted, "Thank you, God!   Thank you!"   Then I leaped into Michael's arms still shouting, "Watch out world, because Michael and I are having a baby!"

Michael swung me around once and shouted, "Yahoo! My baby's having a baby!" Setting my feet on the ground, he lovingly gazed into my eyes, "I love you, and Punkie I don't think I could ever be happier than I am at this very moment." He kissed me deeply, then with tears in his eyes and a broken voice said, "Thank you Christina, for loving me enough to bring me to my senses.   Since we've been back together I can't remember what life was like without you."

I kissed him, "Michael, I love you and I'm so happy I could tell the world."

"I know how you feel Christina, but I think we shouldn't tell anyone until the baby's born."

I looked at him sadly, "You're right.   Damn Michael, we can't tell anyone."

He smiled, "Well one thing I do know we have to tell my Mom, Jimmy and Pierre or they'll never forgive us."

My face lit up again as I said, "We also have to call Barbara Goldstein, she is my steep-mom remember. Why don't we ask them all come for dinner tonight, then we can tell them together."

"That sounds great!   You know they're going to

be shocked."

I laughed then said, "To say the least.   Come on, let's go call them now."   And off we went back to the house like two happy carefree children, anxious to share our good news with the three people closest to us.

That night after dinner Michael and I ended up joyfully telling Tess, Jimmy and his new lover Pierre our good news.   Barbara couldn't make it, the rest did. They went wild with excitement for us at first, especially Tess.   But immediately after the enthusiasm of the moment passed, it was Jimmy who voiced the first concern by saying, "This is fabulous news guys, but aren't you putting yourself in danger?   I thought you weren't going to take that chance again, especially since you nearly died the last time."

Tess interrupted at that point with a powerful, "Oh My God!   Lord Jesus, Mary and Joseph!   Do the two of you know the chance you're taking?"

We both smiled with overwhelming joy radiating on our faces as Michael very calmly said, "Listen guys, we know this may seem extreme.   But what you don't know is both of us believe in our hearts that through the power of prayer and meditation, Christina has tapped into the essence of her oneness with God.   While in these meditative states of oneness, we believe she was able to heal her own wounds from within."

They were all speechless until Tess rose from her seat, came to hug us with open arms and said, "I love you both very much and knowing you both like I do, I know if you truly feel this strongly about this, then so do I. But to play it safe I'm going to be coming up here to help you as much as I can, Christina.   I may be seventy seven, but after 10:00am I can still help with the chores. For some reason God still keeps a lot of life in these old bones and I don't like wasting it."

Forbidden Child III Exposed

I hugged her, smiled and said, "Thank you, Tess. I'm sure as time goes on your help is going to be more than just welcomed."

At that, Jimmy and Pierre echoed her sentiments with warm embraces until I said, "Come on guys, let's go on the deck for dessert; I made cheesecake."

"Cheesecake, that's my favorite." Tess replied cheerfully as she rose from her seat.

"Mine too!" I answered as I headed for the kitchen.

"Punkie," Michael interrupted, "Why don't you take everyone to the deck and let me get dessert?"

"I'll help!" Pierre added as he followed Michael into the kitchen. As they went for our dessert, Tess, Jimmy and I headed for the deck.

As we took our seats Tess lovingly took my hand, "I'm so excited that another Gillespie child will be carried to term in this old house. Did you know I conceived and carried all my children to term in this house?"

"You're kidding!" I said excitedly, "Oh please tell me Tess, where was Michael born?"

She started to laugh then said, "Oh my heavens! I haven't thought about that day in years. Michael was born in Benedictine Hospital in Kingston. Do you mean I never told you the story of Michael's birth?"

"No, you haven't," I replied eagerly.

She smiled and said, "Oh God! You're going to love this story Christina, because that Michael of ours did things his way from day one. I was at the hospital in labor with him for twelve hours and then the labor just stopped. I stayed in the hospital two more days with no pain at all, so I was discharged. Joe, Michael's father started to take me back home and when we made it to the top of the mountain I went back into labor. Joe took off flying back down the mountain and was pulled over by the troopers, who ended up giving us a police escort all the way to the hospital. When we got there the doctor had already left and Michael wasn't about to wait, so he was delivered by a nun named, Sister Genevieve Clare."

"Oh, No," I roared as we all started to laugh.

Just then Michael and Pierre appeared with our dessert. Michael glanced at me tenderly as he began to set the patio table and said, "What are you guys laughing about?"

"You" I chuckled, "Mom was just telling us the 'NOW' legendary story of your birth. It seems you've been a stubborn pain in everybody's ass since the day you decided to grace us with your presence." At that we all laughed.

Michael still gazing at me shook his head with a smile and said, "Normally I'd lambaste you for that one Punkie, but your smile right now is worth all the laughs in the world at my expense. Because you've never appeared more beautiful to me then you do at this very moment."

I began to feel flush by his words when I shyly said, "Oh Michael, that's so sweet I think I'm going to cry." And like a blubbering idiot I did just that. Only the tears flowed so hard that I started to laugh as I tried to say, "I'm sorry, it was just the sweetest thing anyone ever said to me."

Michael knelt down beside me slightly laughing, "I think I better watch what I say to you for a while." With that, we all laughed some more.

From that night on the three of them made it a point to be with Michael and me as much as possible during the entire duration of my pregnancy. It started with them spending the weekends with us. Then in November they came to fix us Thanksgiving Dinner and stayed the whole week, which wasn't too bad; but when they came in December to spend Christmas week with us and didn't leave until the end of January, they were beginning to get on our nerves.   But they meant well, so we said nothing.

In February of 1992, I was nominated for three Grammies, so we decided to take the week before the ceremony to spend it alone with Barbara at her Malibu home.   We enjoyed one very relaxing night with Barbara, and the next morning Jimmy was at the door with Pierre and Tess. They wanted to surprise us and they sure did, by spending the rest of that week with us. At least Tess got to go to her first Grammy Ceremony, where I just happened to win three more Grammies for 'Michael My Love.'   But the worst came when the three of them got together and decided that since my June 16th, due date was closing in; I shouldn't do anything strenuous for the rest of my pregnancy. So on May 1, 1992, forty six days before my due date they all moved in with us. "To help."   As a matter of fact, I was being helped so well, that by June 6th, I cracked. The night before I was so uncomfortable that I didn't fall asleep until sometime after 5:00am, which was bad enough. But when a loud noise startled me awake later that morning, I decided I had, had enough help! So still not feeling well, I flew out of the bed and dashed toward the kitchen, holding my big round, sour belly all the way. When I reached the source of the noise, I found the four of them sitting around the table laughing. About what God knows, all I know is I didn't like it at all and I wasted no time in informing them of that fact when I shouted, "What the hell is wrong with the four of you? Are you trying to scare the baby out of me?"   Directing my words straight at Tess, Jimmy and Pierre I continued, "And you three!   I thought you came to help me, instead you're driving me nuts!"   Now including Michael, I added, "All I hear from the four of you is, don't do that Christina you might hurt yourself, or go lay down Christina you need your rest.   Do I look like an invalid to you people?   Well I'm not!"

Jimmy stood up and calmly replied, "Well, what is it you'd like from us then, Ms. Prima-Donna?"

I gave him my 'don't mess' look and said, "Since you asked so nicely smart ass, it would be nice to have the four of you off my back for just ten minutes."

"Well!"   Tess snapped with indignation as she stood up, "If this is the thanks we get for caring enough to disrupt our whole lives for your welfare, then I think I'll leave for more than ten minutes."   And she started to walk away.

Realizing how I just spoke to the people I loved most in this world, I quickly said, "Tess, please wait!   I didn't mean what I said to any of you.   I love you all and I do know how wonderful you've all been.   So won't you all please forgive me and ignore what I said."

She came over to hug me, "I had five children and I remember what it's like."

Then Michael wrapped his loving arms around me and added, "Would you like us to leave for a while so you can have some free time?"

I smiled softly, "No, honey.   What I'd like is for you to take us all to Pizza Hut for lunch."   Turning to the rest of them I continued, "Who's up for pizza?"

CHAPTER 5

We spent the rest of that beautiful sunny June day driving around the countryside. We had lunch in Albany, dinner in Catskill and didn't get back home until 8:00 that evening. I was so tired when we did get home, I headed straight for the bedroom and in minutes I was fast asleep. Only once again it didn't last. I found myself awake at 1:00am and this time my belly wasn't just sour, it was bursting with pain. I grabbed Michael's arm and shouted, "Oh shit! Michael, wake up! I think it's time!"

He flew out of bed and in ten minutes we were all on our way to Benedictine Hospital in Kingston, N.Y. I was checked in at 1:45am and as far as I was concerned I was already in full blown labor, but to my dismay I was wrong, because the pain only increased as the night grew longer.

It was 4:00am when I was offered a spinal but I refused. I was just as determined to keep my wits about me through this pain, as this child was determined to keep causing the pain. Michael held my hand through every joy filled tear of that very painful labor. Finally around 11:30am, I squeezed his hand extra hard and screamed, "Oh God! It won't be long now."

He wiped the beads of sweat from my brow, kissed my forehead and said, "You can do this Punkie. Just hang in here with me and we'll bring our baby into the world together."

Forbidden Child III Exposed

I chuckled as I cried, "I'm doing just fine, Michael. This is the purest pain I've ever felt and I wouldn't miss it for the world. Ouch!" And at 11:50am, on Sunday, June 7th, 1992, I thankfully heard the first cry of our beautiful new baby. We both started to cry the minute the doctor handed us our five pound thirteen ounce, blonde haired, blue eyed, baby boy. My heart was filled with untamed wonder and joy, as I held our precious bundle of love. I lovingly gazed at Michael who was gazing at his new baby with an expression of divine love on his face, and I thought, 'Thank You, Lord Jesus for granting our prayers and I vow to be the best mother I can possibly be.' Michael gazed up at me and the second his eyes met mine, we both knew this was the happiest moment of our lives. I recovered so quickly, I was back in my private room with the baby by 1:35pm. When we settled in the room, I took Michael's hand and said, "Would you like to hold your son?"

He looked at me with frightened eyes and replied, "He's so small. I won't hurt him will I?"

"No, silly" I chuckled. "Just cuddle him gently in your arms and he'll be fine."

Michael took him and the moment he did his face lit up like a Hollywood Premier as he said, "Christina he's beautiful and he's our little angel."

I watched in pure delight as Michael tenderly held his son and I was grateful to God I was able to give my Michael the son for which he so desperately longed. We had ten minutes alone with our son, before the happy trio came tiptoeing in and as soon as they laid their eyes on him he won their hearts.

"God bless him!" Tess said with tears in her eyes, "He is the most precious little thing I've ever seen."

As for Jimmy, he started crying before he saw the

Forbidden Child III Exposed

baby and it only got worse when he did see him.

Pierre came to hug me and said, "I'm so happy for you boss lady, that's one beautiful baby you just gave birth to."

I kissed his cheek as I replied, "Thank you Pierre, that was sweet and just in case you're not aware of it, I'm very happy you've joined our family. You and Jimmy seem to be meant for each other, and I'm so glad I had something to do with bringing the two of you together."

Just then Doctor Hart entered the room with a slight tap on the door and a big smile, "Well how's that little man doing?"

"Great, Doc."   Michael gleamed back still holding our son.

Doctor Hart patted Michael's back, "I'm glad to hear it.   Have you decided on a name yet?"

Michael turned to me, "I think we've chosen Tyler James, right honey?"

Just as I opened my mouth to answer, Tess said, "Tyler, I thought you were saying Taylor?"

I looked at her with pleasant surprise and said, "Tess, I never even once thought of the name Taylor, but I love it.   Michael let's name him Taylor James Gillespie."

Michael turned toward Doctor Hart as he gazed down at the bundle still in his arms and said, "Welcome to earth, Taylor James Gillespie. I'm your Father, and my name's Michael." Now pointing at me, "You see that angel in the bed over there?   Well she's your mother and her name is Christina." Kissing his forehead, he continued, "Taylor, my boy, there is nothing in the world more precious to either one of us then you little guy. I love you son, and I will always be here for you."

Tess kissed Michael's cheek then said, "Let me hold him please."   With a proud smile, Michael handed

Forbidden Child III Exposed

Taylor to Tess, "Here's your grandson, Nanny."

With tears in her eyes she took Taylor, "He's an angel, Michael." When Jimmy finally managed to stop crying, he hugged me and said, "Great job, girlfriend! He's such a little doll and I'm so happy you'd think he was my son."

I kissed his cheek, "I love you, Uncle Jimmy."

We walked out of the hospital at 10:00am on June 9th, to the largest gathering of international reporters I had seen since my joint news conference with the President. The first thing Taylor James Gillespie did, on the front steps of Benedictine Hospital, was to meet the world. There had to be more photos taken of the three of us that morning then were taken of me all year long. We gave the world a fifteen minute view into our private lives, and then we were helicoptered to our Milton home. From there we eventually managed to slip out of the Powers Compound and we headed right back to our mountain hideaway. It was 6:00pm when we reached the driveway of our home and to my surprise the parking lot was full of cars. I turned to Michael nervously, "Oh no! The Press found us."

"Relax, Punkie!" Michael replied with a calm smile. "It's your in-laws. Since we never told them you were pregnant, they asked to come up tonight to surprise you with a baby shower and meet Taylor at the same time."

My adrenaline stopped flowing as I smiled with relief, "That's nice honey, but Taylor's sleeping and I didn't want him getting too much attention just yet, so if they start to get out of control I want you to say something, all right?"

"All right, but if you're uncomfortable, you can say something. They're your family now too you know."

Forbidden Child III Exposed

"I know, it's just that your siblings think I'm nuts as it is; I don't want them thinking I'm a bitch too."

Starting to laugh he said, "Punkie, I don't care what they think because I know the real you."   Then he kissed me and we headed in.

The family gathering that night turned out to be quite nice.   Especially since I discovered when Michael's siblings weren't busy passing judgement on me, they were actually fun to be with.   But the best was all the wonderfully, thoughtful and creative gifts Taylor received from his new family.   It was the closest experience to a family of my own I had ever known. The love they bestowed on Taylor and I truly made me feel welcomed into the Gillespie clan.   Of course they all doted over Taylor, but not too much, and everyone had the chance to hold him including Michael's sixteen year old niece Michelle.   But the best thing happened when Michael's eldest sister Carol was holding Taylor. She was rocking him in her arms as she walked him back and forth between the living room and dining room. During one of her trips she stopped in the living room where we were all sitting and said, "He's falling asleep Christina, should I put him in his cradle?"   The minute she said cradle, Taylor opened his eyes, looked straight into hers and started to frown.   Carol's face took on a shocked expression as she said, "This kid's is a freaking little genius!"   Laughing, she turned toward Michael, "Little brother, I have a feeling your son is going to show you first hand just what you put Mom and me through when you were his size."

At that Tess joined the laughter then said, "God help you Christina, if Taylor is half the independent spirit Michael was."

I stopped laughing then said, "Tess, chances are Taylor's going to outdo even Michael's childhood reputation and probably by leaps and bounds."

When it was time for everyone to leave I lovingly asked Jimmy and Pierre to leave with them. I asked Tess to stay on with us for the rest of the week. I told her it was because I wanted to draw on her years of experience, but the real reason was I knew it would have broken her heart if I asked her to leave then. And the look on her face as she vowed to help us as long as we needed, said it all. That look, at that moment, was filled with such unconditional love that it went straight to my heart and I knew there would always be a place for her there.

I fed Taylor and had him sleeping nicely by 10:00pm. The three of us spent the next two hours just watching him sleep. It wasn't until midnight that Tess looked at us and whispered, "We better get some sleep before he's ready to eat again, or none of us will be sleeping tonight."

With that she left our room and not two seconds later Taylor was ready to eat. Guess what? Tess was right! None of us did sleep that night, but not for the reasons Tess thought. It was because every time Taylor would fall asleep, one of the three of us would start poking him to make sure he was still breathing. We were so bad that it was the three of us who ended up keeping Taylor up all night, and as for that first night, Tess's years of experience turned out to be quite useless. She was so worried Taylor would slip out of her once strong arms that she was afraid to do anything for him except hold him in the rocking chair and only after she was already seated. But it wasn't until Michael asked her to help us change Taylor's diaper that I knew I was in trouble.

Michael was holding Taylor on the changing stand and while I removed his diaper he said, "Mom, hand us one of those diapers please?" Which I thought was strange since they were two feet from his hand, but I said nothing. Then, Tess put her hand in the diaper bag but she didn't hand us a diaper. She had her back to us as we waited, so we couldn't see what was taking so long. Finally Michael said, "Just hand me one diaper, Mom. That's all."

Her reply was, "These damned fool new diapers, I never saw such a thing." We turned around and Tess had taped both her hands together with one diaper. Michael started to laugh as he grabbed the diaper from her hand; "Give me that Mom and stop fooling around, you silly gooses."

Taylor was now crying as he laid there still waiting for the warmth of a diaper so I said, "Come on guys, where's the diaper already? He's getting cold."

"Hold on it's coming," replied Michael. When I gazed at their reflection in the mirror, I was dumbfounded, for now the two of them where taped to the same diaper and struggling to break free.

I picked Taylor up to stop him from crying, grabbed a new diaper from the other side of the bag their hands were taped to and laughed as I said, "Taylor, honey, whatever you do don't take after your father's side of the family; I'm getting a feeling the whole bunch of them might be silly geese." With that, Michael and Tess both burst into laughter.

We were all so tired when we finally fell asleep that morning, that no one but me heard the banging on the front door. I nudged Michael who was unconscious, looked at the alarm clock and thought, "8:00am, who the hell would be here now?" The banging started again. I climbed out of bed, threw on my robe and headed for the door. When I opened it, Jimmy was standing there with a big smile and a pile of newspapers. I shook my head,

"Come on in, just try to be quiet.   We only fell asleep an hour ago."   As we walked to the kitchen I continued, "What are you doing here this early anyway?"

He placed his bundle on the kitchen table and started to make a pot of coffee as he said, "I wanted to see my nephew, is that all right with you?"

I smiled, "Of course it's all right, smart ass.   It's just that I've been seeing you so much lately, I'm wondering if you're keeping a close enough eye on our little empire."

"Don't you worry about our empire girlfriend, everything's just fine.   You just worry about taking care of your precious family.   Now I don't want to hear any more about where I should be today, because no matter what you say I'm spending the day with Taylor. Besides, Pierre can watch things by himself for one day."

I laughed as I took two cups from the cupboard, "So what's all the papers for?"

"I stopped for coffee on my way up here and yours', Michael's, and Taylor's photos were on the front page of every paper on the rack, so I grabbed every copy of each newspaper they had.   I thought it might be nice for Taylor to someday read what the world had to say about his birth."

I chuckled, "What's he going to do with the rest of them, wallpaper his walls?"   I poured our coffees, took a seat beside Jimmy, picked up the New York Times and started to laugh as I said, "Get this Jimmy! *'Christina Powers* **defies medical advice, as she once again dares to stare into the face of death, to give birth to her now famous son, Taylor James Gillespie!'** Can you believe that?"

"You think that one's bad!"   Jimmy laughed, "Listen to what the Post wrote, '*Christina Powers* **now adds miracles to her list of achievements, as she gave**

birth to her new son, Taylor James Gillespie.'

I laughed again, "I can't believe they actually printed this stuff."

"Oh wait!" Jimmy interrupted. "Here's the Albany Times Union, **'Christina and Michael bask in their love as they proudly introduce their beautiful new son, Taylor James Gillespie to a cheering public'.**"

"Wow! That was really sweet," I said. "I think I'll drop the reporter a card." That's when Taylor started calling.

Tess stayed with us for the rest of that week, and there wasn't a moment that she didn't spend doting over Taylor. She adored him and it warmed my heart to see what a loving grandmother Taylor truly had.

As for Jimmy and Pierre, they came up every night after work and of course Jimmy brought a new stuffed animal with him each time. The only difference when Jimmy and Pierre came up for dinner that Friday night was Jimmy informed us they were staying for the weekend. We didn't argue, we knew better, and I was actually glad they did because we ended up having a great time. It was around 10pm Friday night when we all decided to retire for the night. I woke up at 1am and could not fall back to sleep; so, I thought I'd go wake Jimmy and ask him to make some of his famous buttered popcorn. I made my way to the room he and Pierre were sleeping in, and when I opened the bedroom door I was surprised to find Jimmy standing on the bed with a huge erection and his legs spread eagle directly over Pierre who was laying on his back beneath him totally nude saying, "Oh baby, you are my Colossus of Rhodes!"

I started to laugh so hard and the moment they realized I was there, Jimmy screamed, lost his balance and fell off the bed hitting the back of his head on the dresser as Pierre frantically tried to cover himself.

"Oh my God!" I shouted as I ran to Jimmy's aid struggling not to laugh. "Are you alright?"

Holding the back of his head he yelled, "Ouch that hurts! What the hell is wrong with you girlfriend, did you forget how to knock?" He then looked up at me and started to laugh, "My fucking genius is back. What great idea did you get this time?"

That's when Michael came charging into the room yelling, "What the hell's going on?"

I looked at the three of them and started to laugh so hard I almost couldn't get the words out as I said, "I just wanted to ask Jimmy to fix me some of his famous buttered popcorn."

Pierre joined the laughter as he wrapped the sheet around his waist, hopped out of the bed and said, "Great idea Christina, that's just want I was about to ask Jimmy to do when you entered the room." Turning to Jimmy he continued, "Is our popcorn ready yet?"

Jimmy, now putting on his shorts added, "Great, now I have two fucking geniuses to deal with." He looked towards Michael; "Come on Mike, let's go fix our geniuses some popcorn or neither one of us is ever going to get some sex tonight."

We all laughed some more as we went downstairs and ate two big bowls of the best buttered popcorn in the world. But the best thing that happened that weekend came after our Sunday night dinner, when Michael brought out six cupcakes with a birthday candle in each one and said, "These are to celebrate Taylor's first week's birthday. Now we're going to sing happy birthday to Taylor and as we blow our candles out, we can make our own special wish just for him."

With a surprised expression I said, "That's

beautiful, honey."

After our little party, Jimmy said, "This was a great idea Michael, why don't we throw Taylor another birthday party next weekend?"

"I'll tell you what," Michael replied with a gentle smile. "Why don't we all plan to spend next weekend together?" When everyone agreed Michael added, "Listen up guys, Christina and I have to ask all three of you to stay home this week. We need some time alone, just the three of us, all right?"

Reluctantly they all agreed and when they left that night, it was actually the first time Michael, Taylor and I were alone together, since Taylor's birth. It was such an incredible experience being alone as a family that night, that all Michael and I could do was lovingly bask in the wondrous feelings of parenthood. We were both so happy we couldn't keep the smiles from our faces if we tried, especially since every little movement Taylor made gave us another reason to smile. As the days passed that summer, we had to be the happiest little family in the entire world.

Every time Michael picked Taylor up, he glowed with a divine love for his son and wife. As for me, I was finally a Mom again and somehow the precious gift of motherhood made me feel complete as a woman and a wife. I finally had my angel and what an angel he was. He would sleep all night long and he never cried unless he was wet or hungry. He was such a happy baby and every smile he gave me told me so. He wrapped my heart around his tiny finger a little tighter with every smile, especially when I would sing to him. I sang a new song to him straight from my heart every time I would feed him. He was the only person in the world who could get me to start singing with a smile, and his smile radiated the deepest feeling of unconditional love I had ever known.   As for his little birthday Parties, well they became a weekly occurrence with cake, wrapped presents and all the party favors.   The five of us loved Taylor so much that he just became the center of all our lives.   If Michael and I had let them, Tess, Jimmy, and Pierre would have moved in with us for good.

CHAPTER 6

Our lives' were going along wonderfully that summer right up until September 22nd, 1992; until Jimmy called me at 11:00am and said, "Christina, I just received a call from President Rush, who asked me to please have you call him as soon as possible. He sounded as if it was urgent and he said for you to call him on his private line."

I thanked him then told Michael who said, "Whatever he wants, you talk to me before you say anything, all right?"

I smiled as I answered, "Yes, sir." Then I picked up the phone and proceeded to dial the President's number. When he answered, I said, "Hi, George, Jimmy told me you called and he said it sounded urgent. Is something wrong?"

"Thanks for calling so promptly Christina; I've always appreciated that in you. Now to answer your question, yes there is something wrong and I'm calling to ask for your help."

"What is it?" I asked with concern.

"Christina, I've been slipping in the polls steadily over the last three months and its dramatic enough to cause me great concern. That's why I'm now asking you and Michael to come with the baby and make a cameo appearance at the Republican Convention in Dallas tomorrow night. It's the last night of the convention Christina and it needs a shot in the arm. I believe if you were both to endorse my campaign while holding Taylor in your arms; then, the tide of the election could be turned back in my direction."

With a surprised tone I answered, "George, I'm flattered you think Michael and I have that much influence with the American public, but I really think the voters are going to vote on the issues, no matter what we may say."

"Are you kidding, Christina? Right now the three of you are America's most famous family. The American people love you and all the public opinion polls show that you are the most trusted public figure since President Kenney. I'm telling you people will listen to what you have to say Christina, especially if the two of you back me as a family. Won't you please help me? All I'm asking is for you to read a two minute speech at the convention, with Michael holding Taylor beside you. Christina, you know I'd do anything for you and I'm only asking for one night out of your time."

"Listen George, let me speak with Michael and I'll get back to you."

The moment I told Michael the details of my conversation with George, he outright refused by saying, "There is no way I'm parading my family on national television to support him, especially when I have no intentions of voting for him myself. Christina, can't you see from the last time we had to deal with him that he's just trying to use us? On the outside the man comes across like a great guy, but I don't trust him and if I don't trust him there's no way I'm going to publicly support him."

"Michael, I agree with you completely and if I hadn't given my word I'd support his reelection campaign, I would have never done so in the first place. But since I did give jmy word to support him I feel obligated to go. So, for the honor of my word honey, I'm asking you to allow me to go by myself to do this one

Forbidden Child III Exposed

more thing for him."

He shook his head and said, "I've learned not to fight with you when you're right Punkie; so, if you really want to go then your family is coming with you. Just don't expect Taylor and I, to take center stage with you when you read whatever 'bull' it is he wants you to pawn off on the public." The next morning the three of us were on our way to the Republican Convention in Dallas, Texas, which also happened to be George's hometown.

It was 7:00pm when we entered the convention hall with the President's immediate party and as we walked to our seats we were cheered by the crowd so loudly, the noise had Taylor crying in seconds. I was able to calm him down as the stadium quieted, then we proceeded to sit through two hours of Republican indoctrination. The first half hour went to the vice-president who touted the Administration's achievements over the last four years. The next speaker was Republican Majority Leader, my ex-husband Lee Bradford. Lee spent an entire hour virtually spouting out the trustworthiness of the current administration and the faithful determination of the Republican Party to steadfastly stand for the morality of the American family. By the time Lee finished his speech, I was nearly nauseous and that's when Reverend Truewell took the podium. The good Reverend took the next fifteen minutes to praise the virtues of the return of family values in the United States. He dedicated the next fifteen minutes on rebuking the evils of the Democratic Party, by starting with their plans to allow gays in the military. After that he condemned them as well for their refusal to overturn Roe v. Wade. Incredibly I was able to hold my anger until he said, "What will they want next, for us to recognize the rights of homosexuals to marry and adopt children.   That's not the type of family God wants raising our children, and as long as the Holy Bible say's in Leviticus 20:13, '**If a man lies with another man they are an abomination and shall be put to death.**' And that is why we must never allow the evils of the Democratic Party to prevail."

He proceeded to sum up his sermon with a prayer for victory and that's when the announcer said, "Ladies and gentleman, to introduce the President we have invited some special guests here tonight. So without further delay, I'd like to welcome America's most popular family, Christina, Michael, and Taylor Powers Gillespie."

Cheers filled the stadium as Michael grabbed my arm and said, "Damn it Christina, I told him Taylor and I weren't to be announced with you, and I'm not taking him up there."

I looked desperately into his eyes as I pleaded in a whisper, "Michael, Please, come up there with me or I won't be able to do this."

"No!" He grunted back.

I pleaded again, "Michael, I need you! Please do this for me, not for him?"

With that he took Taylor from my hands as he stood up and with anger in his voice said, "I'm only doing this for you, so let's get it over with."   And off we nervously headed toward the podium.

We were both smiling as we stood before the cameras and my smile immediately turned into a look of horror, as I glanced at the monitor in front of me which read, **"Good Evening, America!   I must first say that Michael, Taylor and I are honored to be here tonight. We have come as an American family to give our full support to the President's bid for reelection and the Republican Party's Commitment to uphold the**

honest Christian family values of all American citizens." I just stood there speechless. I couldn't bring myself to say anything, no less read those words.

Michael brought me out of my momentary coma with a nudge to my arm and the moment I regained my composure I said, "Please forgive me, but in good conscience I cannot read the words on the monitor." I quickly turned behind me, toward where George was seated and looked him dead in the eyes. Then I turned back toward the audience and with disgust in my voice added, "I'm sorry George, but after having listened to such hypocrisy, I must withdraw my support for your campaign."

That's when the delegates gasped from shock and little did they know I was only getting started, "What gives any of you the right to think you can dictate American morality? Do you all really believe having some puffed up preacher stand here on National TV advocating the hatred and discrimination of millions of innocent people, is truly the type of leadership our country needs? Well personally I don't think so. I think we're looking for real leadership, the kind that will bring our nation together not divide it."

Everyone there was still gasping for breath when Reverend Truewell grabbed a mike on the other side of the stage and said, "You're no longer welcomed here, Ms. Powers! You have blasphemed the Holy Word of God, by calling my scripture reading hypocrisy, so please leave."

"I'm leaving sir!" I answered with my head held high, "But not because I've blasphemed anything. It's because I'm getting sick to my stomach from just being here. Can't you see that you're the one who is the blasphemer? How can you proclaim the love of Christ in one breath, and then condemn your brothers in another

Forbidden Child III Exposed

breath?   You quote death from a book you call Holy and you ignore the fact that Christ died on a cross to free us from the sin that you and that book, are so willing to chain us all back up to. Reverend I've searched my thoughts while you preached from your Holy Bible, and for the life of me; I couldn't find one Holy Word in your entire sermon."

With indignation he shouted, "How dare you question my knowledge of why Christ was crucified, especially when it's evident you have no idea what Christ died for?"

Calmly I replied, "Reverend, I'm not going to argue scripture with you or defend my statements, because until people like yourself understand that all Christ wants from us is to follow his example, and not the laws of the Old Testament, then it would do no good."

With that he screamed at me, "Are you now telling me to disregard the Bible, which everyone knows is the Holy Word of God?"

Still holding my composure I answered, "I don't think you should just disregard the Bible reverend, I think we should throw it away! Along with all the negative concepts that come along with it, like prejudice, hatred, bigotry, and murder. Can't you see that the world would be a much better place if we just followed Christ's teachings of unconditional love and nailed the rest of the book back on The Cross where Christ intended for it to go nearly two thousand years ago?"

At that everyone began to boo me and the good reverend lost it all together as he started to shout, "The entire world knows you're nothing but a harlot and you dare to preach to me?"

That's when Michael grabbed the mike and said, "Sir, if I weren't a gentleman I'd make you eat those words, but since I am I'll take my family and just leave. And, Sir! For your own good, I hope you can be civil enough to keep your crude remarks to yourself." Then he put the mike down, took my hand and said, "Come on honey, let's get out of this God forsaken place."

The reaction of the spectators was pure anger. We were booed and sneered at so badly as we headed out of the auditorium, that even the President himself couldn't calm the crowd down fast enough. And that wasn't the worst, for when we tried to leave the building the mob outside began throwing bottles and stones at us. Michael quickly closed the door and ushered us back to the security office to seek help. When we were inside, I turned to Michael and said, "I'm sorry, Michael. I had no idea people would react like this when I said what I did, but I was so angered by the stupidity of their doctrine that I had to speak out."

He hugged me reassuringly and said, "Don't be sorry Christina, if you hadn't said something I would have."

Just then the President entered the room and in an angry tone said, "The mob out front has become so unruly, the Governor has had to call in an extra hundred and fifty Riot Control Officers. It will probably take half the night to quiet the damn city down. What the hell were you thinking?"

"Hold on Mr. President." Michael interrupted. "If you would like us to continue this conversation, then please speak in a civil tone, because there is no reason for you to speak to anyone like that."

"Well excuse me, Mr. Powers," George snapped back sarcastically. "That's because you're not the one who's Presidential reelection chances, have just been blown to hell on National TV." With that he took two deep breaths and after calming himself for a moment he shook his head as he looked at me and added, "I could have gracefully accepted the public withdrawal of your support from my campaign, but how do I publicly accept your all-out assault on the entire Republican Platform?"

I returned his steady gaze with a look of sincerity and said, "George, I don't know if you can understand this, but I was compelled to say what I did."

Without blinking he replied, "Your security chief has your helicopter waiting on the roof to take the three of you safely to Houston. I'm afraid you'll have to fly out of Texas from there. It seems there's already a mob waiting for you at the Dallas Airport, with protest signs which read, **'Death to the Fag Lovers!'** And **'Let's keep the Bible and nail Christina Powers to the cross!'** So I think it would be wise for you to leave town now. There's an armed guard waiting in the hall to take you to the roof." Then, he turned to walk out and when he reached the door he turned back and added, "Oh by the way Christina, I don't know if you can understand this, but I'm now compelled to publicly destroy you." And with that he exited the room.

It was 10:00 the following morning when our jet taxied down at Stewart Airport and we were greeted by another large gathering of protesters. Only this time, they were divided into two groups, with half of them cheering a chant, "Way to go, Christina! That's why we love you!" The other half was booing a chant, "Down with the Anti-Bible fagot lovers."

As we exited the plane, we were ushered by thirty or so, New York State Police Officers past the crowd and straight into a bee hive of reporters. They shouted questions as we walked past and in the midst of this madness I turned to Michael and said, "Michael, if I don't make a public statement right now in defense of my actions, it will look as though I'm ashamed of what I said."

He stopped us dead in our tracks and said, "Well you better start talking to them then. Because I'll be damned, before I'll let the world think you're anything but proud of what you said." He shouted to the reporters, "If you will all just calm down and ask your question's one at a time, then we'll be more than happy to answer them." Right on that spot, we began to hold a mini press conference, while Taylor fell asleep in Michael's arms.

The first question asked was, "Christina, some of your critics are saying you have disgraced yourself by what they see as a deliberate attempt to sabotage the President's reelection campaign, and the reputation of the Republican Party. Would you care to comment on those charges at this time?"

"If the critics you speak of, think making a stand against injustice, wherever it may be found is disgraceful, then as far as I'm concerned, their opinions are worthless. And as for the validity of the insinuation that my actions were premeditated to sabotage the President, or the Republican Party's reputation in any way, is absolutely ludicrous."

"Christina! Christina!" Asked the hungry mob of reporters until I took the next question by pointing, "Christina, the world's Christian community is up in arms over your controversial statements that the world would be a better place without the Bible and it should be thrown away. At this time would you care to respond to their outrage, as well as shed further light on what you meant when you said and I quote, 'The Bible should be nailed back on the cross where Christ intended it to be in the first place?'"

I smiled at the young reporter then gently said, "My words weren't meant to be taken literally. I spoke as Christ himself might have, in a parable. What was meant by the parable had nothing to do with crucifying the Bible. I was simply stating when Christ died; He took the penalty of sin and the laws of sin to the cross with him. I'm just so sick of the spiritual leaders of today, thinking it's their responsibility to continue to keep the world enslaved to the laws of the Bible's Old Testament. Especially when they should be freeing the world from the laws of the Bible and the knowledge of sin that comes with it, like Christ taught us to do. For didn't Christ himself say in Matthew 15:9, '**But, in vain they do worship me, teaching for doctrines of man.**' Christ also taught in Matthew 7:1, '**Judge not, that ye be not judged.**' The reason I said what I did is because history has shown us that man has been using the laws of the Bible and all the Sacred Books to justify war, prejudice and murder for centuries now, and all in the name of God and through the laws of The Old Testament, New Testament, Torah and the Quran. Well I think it's time we stopped all the judging and leave the job of conviction and self-judgement up to the Holy Spirit. For Christ didn't tell us to follow the laws of the Old Testament, because He fulfilled them when He also said in Matthew 26:56, '**But all this was done, that the scriptures of the prophets might be fulfilled.**' He said again in Matthew 28:20, '**Teaching them to observe all things whatsoever I have commanded.**' Not the Old Testament's commandments. What Christ commanded can again be found in Matthew 22:37-40, '**Thou shalt love the Lord thy God with all thy heart and thou shalt love thy neighbor as thyself. On these two Commandments hang all the laws and the prophets.**' And that is why when I heard an entire political party advocating conformity to one belief, it reminded me of the Nazi Regime and I had to speak out."

Forbidden Child III Exposed

"Christina! Christina!" They pleaded again so I pointed and said, "I'll answer one more question."

"Christina, do you plan to support the Democratic Party's nominee for President now that you've withdrawn your support from the President's Campaign?"

I gave a big smile for that one and said, "I think I'll try to stay out of the political scene from now on. Besides, American citizens are smart enough to see past all the smoke screens of both Party's and come straight to the heart of the issues for themselves. That's why I have full confidence the voters will vote with their hearts and minds just fine without my help. Now I'd like to thank everyone for keeping the volume down so Taylor could remain sleeping. It's not many news conferences an infant can sleep through and as a family, we truly appreciate it." At that, we headed for the limo and our State Police Escort to our Milton Home.

Before that interview, I was ridiculed by a majority of Americans', who felt I crossed the lines on freedom of speech and good taste by my actions. After that interview, the opinion polls began to change and no matter how hard the entire Republican Party from the President down tried to slander my character they failed. It appeared that the majority of American citizens now overwhelmingly approved of my public chastising of the President and the Republican Party. It took about two weeks for things to settle down enough for us to sneak back home to our little piece of heaven in The Catskill Mountains. That's when we decided to put the whole nightmarish ordeal behind us and get back to the business at hand, which was simply to live our lives' as loving parents.

CHAPTER 7

Cherished so much was the precious gift we had prayed so hard for, our beautiful new baby boy, Taylor James Gillespie, that we made a conscious choice to finally free ourselves from the complications of the world and the insanity that accompanies it. We didn't even appear publicly when the President angrily blamed me for his loss in the election and thanks to the great work of my Security Chief, Frank Rossi our true whereabouts were never discovered by anyone. As far as the world knew, we were hiding out at our very secure home on the Power's Complex Grounds in Milton, N.Y., but in reality we were in the mountains learning to live a normal family life and loving every second of it. From that time on we devoted our full attentions to Taylor, who was developing into a unique little individual right in front of our eyes. Before we realized it, the days turned into weeks and the weeks into months, and raising Taylor turned out to be the most rewarding aspect of our entire lives. Unbelievably, the eternal love we already had for him somehow grew deeper with every breath we took together. He was so loved and lovable that Michael and I knew there was nothing in this world we wouldn't do for our Taylor. Those sentiments were not just ours either, because Tess, Jimmy, and Pierre were just as devoted to Taylor as we were. The five of us loved him so much that we continued to celebrate his birthday every week for the rest of that year. It wasn't until after his first birthday party that I insisted on cutting the mini birthday Party's down to once a month. The poor little guy's room was becoming so filled with the gifts he was brought every week; it was either cut the Party's or build an addition. I opted for the Party's figuring it would be less strenuous then an addition.

Taylor was a remarkable child to watch grow and he never ceased to amaze us. He actually spoke his first word on his sixth month birthday and of course it was, "Dada." I laughed when he said it and said, "Oh well! I guess Mama will have to settle for second." The next morning over breakfast, I was talking with Jimmy as he spoon-fed Taylor and to the surprise of us all, Taylor reached out to Jimmy and said, "Meme."

We all stopped everything we were doing and when he said it a second time, I leaned my head next to the high chair and said, "Meme! What about Mama?" At that moment he stuck his little tongue out at me and went, "Blppppp" splattering baby cereal right in my face and when he topped it off with a great big grin I lost it.   I started laughing so hard I almost fell off my chair. Needless to say, from that day forth, Jimmy became known as Meme.

The following weekend he stunned us all again with his mastery of the English Language by calling Tess, "Nana." Then on December 19th, 1992, he woke up crying at 2:00am and as I rocked him in my arms he gazed his sleepy eyes up into mine, and with the sweetest voice I ever heard said, "Mama." I looked down at my angel as he struggled to keep his eyes open, and the happiest tears I ever cried began flowing from my eyes. Surprisingly before his seventh month, our little genius had mastered four words.

By his tenth month Taylor was taking his first steps and talking like a toddler. He also turned out to be

Forbidden Child III Exposed

an advanced child athletically and was running around the house like a trooper by his first birthday.   He was so clever that at eighteen months he realized he was the center of our lives, and from that moment on it took him no time to figure out how to get around every one of us. The child was so good with getting his way he could persuade us to do almost anything for him, like racing rocking horses across the living room floor, or marching behind him in single file around the coffee table while playing his harmonica.   He would have Jimmy, I mean Meme, behind him rattling his key chain.   Pierre was next clinking two spoons together.   Then came Dada clanging two pot lids like cymbals and I had to follow up the rear singing Old Macdonald, while Nanny sat in the middle of this marching band around the coffee table. He loved to play and he could turn anything we were doing into a game and have us all laughing hysterically in seconds.

It was hard for all of us not to spoil him by bringing him some little toy every time we went out because he loved getting surprises so much; it was worth a little spoiling. His face would light up every time he opened a gift, but the brightest face of all shown when he came downstairs on Christmas morning 1993, to find a large gift wrapped in red Christmas paper, with golden ribbons and bows all over it. He started opening it very slowly at first, but when he saw there was a shiny white, Volkswagen Convertible just his size hidden by the paper; his face outshone the Christmas tree. He began to tear the paper off so fast and wild, that the automatic camera couldn't snap the picture's fast enough. By his second birthday he was driving that little buggy so well, that Michael and I had to jog just to keep up with him.

At age two and a half our loveable little man, learned that if he didn't get something when he wanted it, he could demand it by throwing a little tantrum. That was a trying six months for all of us let me tell you. But we got through it and by age three he realized negotiating for what he wanted worked better than the tantrums. By three and a half our little monkey was working computer programs better than I could. He actually taught me how to pull up the phone on the computer and make a call while still working on his program. He said and I quote, "I had to call Nanny to say goodnight, but I wasn't finished with my program yet, so I figured I'd do them both at the same time."

I was amazed at his statement so I kissed his cheek and replied, "I love you, my monkey punkie doodle, and I swear you're a little genius."

By the time he turned four our little angel was holding intellectual conversations with us as if he were twelve years old. He loved words so much, he would pick out every new one he heard and if he discovered a word that caught his fancy like "Stupidity," you heard it over and over again accompanied by laugher. This would continue until he understood exactly how to fit the word into as many sentences as he could possibly think of.

Taylor was not only a sweet loving little genius, he was also the most tenderly emotional child I had ever known. Once we found a bird nest laying on the ground with four little blue eggs in it. He picked it up and when he noticed two of them were broken, he started to cry so hard I had to promise to try and save the other two eggs just to calm him down. We ended up taking the nest with the two unbroken eggs home with us to try to hatch them under a light bulb. The eggs hatched two weeks later and the next thing James knew Taylor had two robins' following him everywhere he went. Then there was the incident when we found a trapped field mouse that we had to set free.   When he decided he wanted a dog, we were immediately off to a pet shop where amongst thirty or so puppies he instantly spotted a little ball of white fur and said, "That's the one Dad!   He loves me."   He picked the little Bichon up then turned to Michael and I and smiled as he said, "His name is Pettoe and he wants to come home with me."   So of course, Pettoe came home with us.   Then, he and his two little buddies from down the road Andy, and A.J., would chase Pettoe all over the house.

I always thought I knew the meaning of hard work, but no work I had ever done compared to cleaning up after Michael, Taylor, two birds and a puppy. Between being a mother and a wife, came all the cooking and cleaning.   It didn't take me long to realize one had to be a super woman to be a good mother in the nineties, and I wasn't even holding down a full-time job like most mothers were doing.   Even with all the work I only had to see Taylor smile once a day and it was all worth it.

Everything we did was done as a family, and Taylor was never left out of the decision making.   It got to the point any time Michael or I had to go out of the house without him; we had to inform him of our entire itinerary.   If by chance either one of us were heading to the office for the day, we weren't going alone.   Taylor would start crying with such dramatics to come with us, it would have broken our hearts not to have taken him. After the third crying bout over wanting to come to work with us, we decided the obvious solution was simply to just take him.   Once we got there, it would only take two minutes for his shyness to dissipate, and then he went straight to work running the show and captivating the hearts of all our employees. Of course, he would immediately claim Jimmy who was now being called 'Meme' by everyone, as his business partner and within

Forbidden Child III Exposed

ten minutes the two of them would be working on some major project that Meme would dream up, while Michael and I held board meetings in the same room. I guess it was acceptable to our business associates because no one ever complained about the background noise provided by Taylor and Meme. After a while we thought it was great having Taylor attending our meetings with us. It was actually quite nice being able to keep an eye on him at the same time. After all, he and Meme would play through the meetings anyway, so how could it hurt? It never even crossed our minds he could possibly be taking in the details of each meeting. But on June 11th, 1996, we discovered that was exactly what he was doing, when he came up to me after what was a very stressful board meeting, where I had given hell to the entire top management of one of my subsidiaries and said, "Whoa, you're so cool Mom. It was pure genius the way you handled that meeting."

I looked at him with wide eyes and with a big smile said, "Why thank you, honey." Then I picked him up, kissed his cheek and whispered, "You're the real genius in this family partner, and don't you ever forget it."

Michael, Taylor and I had to be the happiest family on the face of the earth and our family included Nana, Meme and Pierre as well. This happy little boy was so much the center of all our hearts that we shared equally in Taylor's love whenever we were together, and he had more than enough love to go around. Taylor had a way of making every day come alive with new and exciting challenges. He filled our lives with so much love and made those days truly the happiest and peaceful times of my life. Only as everyone knows, all good things must come to an end, and ours ended very abruptly at 10:00 am on July 1st. 1996.

CHAPTER 8

Michael and I had just sat for a meeting with our attorney Tom Davies, who unknowingly brought with him; along with a number of documents to be signed, the final missing pieces to our ever deepening puzzle. I signed where needed then passed the documents to Michael for his signature. As Michael signed the documents, I began going through the latest puzzle pieces. I was carefully examining the information gathered by Tom when I noticed a date on a government contract which was signed by Lee Bradford. The date was March 18th. 1979, and all at once it hit me and I thought, "That's the same date I met Lee and if I'm not mistaken it's also the same date of the last entry on the disc I switched on Lee."

With this in mind I took the disc from my safe and for what had to be the hundredth time, I inserted the disk into my computer. Once I confirmed the date I thought, "I must have tried a thousand different passwords, it couldn't be that simple, could it?" At that I typed in *Christina* and for the first time in seventeen years I was granted access. As the information saved on that disc appeared on the screen, I was shocked to see detailed diagrams of NASA's Space Shuttle. Then all of a sudden on the bottom of the screen appeared the words: 'To access top-level clearance files' type in your six digit password.' As I pondered what this meant I thought, "Oh well, give it a shot." So I typed in

'Powers' and sure enough, the computer responded. After a second look just to make sure my eyes weren't deceiving me, I shouted out in a disgusted tone, "National Security my ass!   The bastard was just covering his own ass."

Michael and Tom immediately stopped what they were doing and at the same time anxiously said, "What is it?"

I had a look of shock on my face as I gazed up at them both and said, "Only proof of the most horrendous crime ever to be perpetrated against the American people." Their faces turned white as they realized the implications of my discovery.

After filling them in on exactly what shocking bit of information we had uncovered, the three of us began to agonize over how to proceed from this point. The first half hour we tossed around the pros and cons over whether revealing this information to the nation at this point, would really be in America's best interest or not. Especially since two of the people involved, were now running for President and vice-president on the Republican ticket.

As we brain-stormed, Tom spoke up, "Let me play devil's advocate for a moment." Looking straight at me he continued, "Christina, I hope you realize if you do expose this conspiracy, you will be opening up a can of worms that has the potential of coming back to haunt us all. There are also a lot of fanatics out there who might want to make us all the targets of an assassin's bullet for exposing this."

I knew exactly what he was saying, so I looked at them both very seriously and said, "I think we have a responsibility to see justice prevails whenever a crime is committed, but I'm not sure I'm willing to go to the point of jeopardizing any of our lives for my beliefs."

Forbidden Child III Exposed

With frustration Michael shook his head at me and said, "Damn Christina, I don't know either! Part of me says we have to come forward with this evidence and the other part say's to just forget it and let sleeping dogs lie. We're not just talking about the three of us you know; we could be putting Taylor in harm's way as well."

That's when Tom said, "The other thing to consider is how high up the political ladder this goes, we don't even know if there is anyone we can trust to tell this to."

Michael's face showed the anguish of our dilemma as he added, "If we don't even know who we can trust to tell the truth to, then I'm not sure how to handle this."

With that we were at a stalemate. Taylor who was playing with Jimmy on the other side of the room, came over to us with a look of pure innocence on his face and from out of the blue said, "Mom, you told me I should always tell the truth and if I make a mistake or do something wrong, I should never be afraid of telling you no matter what it is.   Well I think if these men are afraid to tell you what they did, then you need to let them know it's all right to tell the truth."   I smiled at him lovingly as he looked at Michael and continued, "And Dad, if you don't know who to tell the truth to, then why not just tell everyone the truth, like you told me I should always do?"

Michael snatched him up into his arms and said, "You're right Taylor, that is what I said and that's exactly what we are going to do."   Then he kissed Taylor as he placed him down and continued, "I love you Taylor, and you're the best son in the whole world. Now I want you to go and play with Meme while we finish our meeting."   As Jimmy led Taylor back to their playing, Michael turned to me and said, "We have to go

Forbidden Child III Exposed

public with this, Christina."

I smiled my approval, then taking on a determined expression I said, "You're absolutely correct Michael, we do have to go public and it must be done swiftly and strategically."

CHAPTER 9

Once the decision was made to go all the way to a congressional hearing with this, I figured the safest way to proceed would be by covering our own ass's right from the start. So the first thing we did was have numerous copies made of all the documented proof I had obtained over the years, which collaborated my allegations. Once that was completed, we calculated the time we could have each copy simultaneously hand delivered to their destinations and came up with 7:00pm. Each copy was then sealed in separate briefcases and by 1:10pm on their way out of our office by individual couriers. As soon as word reached us that each courier was safely in the air and on their way to their prospective recipients, I called for a press conference to be held at Powers Inc. for precisely 7:00pm that evening. The rest of that afternoon was spent frantically brainstorming over how to present my case to the American public, without appearing guilty myself.

At that point, Tom convinced me that I would have to alter my story just a bit to cover up the reason I chose to release this information the first time which happened to be the same day of my Wall Street incident in order to protect myself and my family. Otherwise I stood to incriminate myself for 'Insider Trading.' After reluctantly agreeing it was time to put our story together.

It was only two minutes before confronting a conference room full of reporters, which I realized by sheer coincidence our 7:00pm news conference just happened to correspond with the major networks national news broadcasts. So when I stood before those reporters and their cameras, I knew once I started speaking, they would have my image beaming live into the living rooms of the entire nation. That knowledge caused my voice to crack as I said, "Good evening' {cough!} Please excuse me." I cleared my voice, smiled and continued, "Let me try that again."

With that, a friendly laughter filled the room which immediately caused me to relax, just enough to proceed with confidence as I said, "First, I'd like to thank you all for coming and I promise this won't be boring. Next, I respectfully request you refrain from all questions or outbursts, until I have completed my entire statement." I stopped for a sip of water then continued, "Now that, that's out of the way we may begin. As I speak there will be copies of documents passed out to each one of you. These copies are exact duplicates of files, which have been sent to the President and the heads of the FBI and CIA. These files hold documented proof of the allegation I am about to make of conspiracy and treason, against our nation by top officials of our own government."

Instantly the room became filled with shouts of questions from the shocked reporters as they all scrambled to be the first to go live. Once I regained control of the press conference, I continued by saying, "If you will recall, on November 14th, 1981, there was a congressional hearing called to investigate the current Republican Vice Presidential Candidate, Republican Majority Leader, Senator Lee Bradford. This investigation was ordered by the Ways and Means Committee six months after Senator Edward Kenney, made allegations of a conspiracy between the then, Head of NASA, Dan Pigeon and the President of Bradford Computers, Lee Bradford.

The charges alleged that the current Republican Presidential Candidate and Former vice-president Dan Pigeon, had conspired with Lee Bradford for financial kickbacks, before ever awarding the entire computer manufacturing contract, for the space shuttle to Bradford Computers. Bradford Computers was awarded this astounding, one hundred billion dollar, government project in 1975, and since Senator Bradford once worked for NASA as one of the main designers on NASA's own computer programs, Senator Kenney had many questions he wanted answered, concerning possible improprieties.

In an attempt to head off an investigation, Dan Pigeon still heading NASA at the time, then canceled the Bradford Computers contract and awarded it to Peach Computers and Victory Technologies. At the time Senator Kenney made his accusations, I was married to Senator Bradford and knowing him, I did not believe it possible for him to be involved in a conspiracy. However, because Lee Bradford miscalculated the response of his fellow Senate members, I discovered differently.

Since the contract between NASA and Bradford Computers had been canceled, Lee never expected a congressional hearing to be called; thus, when it did it caught him off guard. Fortunately for the Senator, news of the hearing came to his attention the night before it was made public. He was informed that a Federal Marshal was to arrive at 8:00am the following morning to seize all of Bradford's business and personal financial records. That very night certain documents, along with a computer disc belonging to my now ex-husband Senator Lee Bradford, came into my possession. Lee told me the documents were for a secret new computer he was designing and he asked me to keep them in hiding until he needed them. I did as he asked and after he was cleared of all charges from the Congressional Hearing, he asked for them back. I thought it odd and I became concerned I may have inadvertently helped conceal evidence of a crime, so I made copies of everything before returning them to Bradford. I had no idea what these documents contained, because they were in a seemingly undetectable computer generated code, but I knew I had to decode the message if I was ever to know the truth."

With that I thought, 'Lord, forgive me,' as I proceeded to lie through my teeth to cover my ass. I honestly had no idea what the code meant until I finally deciphered the first line which was simply one word, Christina. When I loaded the disc and typed my own name into my computer, I found myself entering NASA's top secret main computer through a built in back door. This discovery was made on December 1st, 1988, when I obtained ownership of Bradford Computers. The following day I informed Senator Kenney of my discovery. He immediately called for a second Congressional Investigation of Senator Bradford, only this time it was on charges of treason and espionage. Before I could get copies of these documents and the disc to Senator Kenney, I was nearly killed by a gunshot wound. The investigation was then placed on hold, until I was well enough to come forward with my evidence. Only the very night I was released from the hospital, I was requested by the then, newly elected President George Rush, to turn the evidence I had over to him. He informed me the information I had would become a threat to national security if it was made public. He wanted me to turn the true documents over to him and turn a phony set of documents over to Senator Kenney. I did as the President requested and gave him what he believed was the only copy of these documents and the disc in existence. Then I turned the phony documents over to Senator Kenney and the following day Senator Bradford was once again cleared of all charges.

After turning the evidence over to the President I never mentioned it again. I decided instead to begin doing some very subtle investigating of my own. I then acquired the assistance of my attorney Tom Davies, who for the last eight years persistently gathered the puzzle pieces to what was clearly unfolding into some sort of political conspiracy. Then at 10:00am this very morning the puzzle was finally completed, and I understood the gravity of the crime committed against our nation and her people. The folders you have received contain dated, documented proof of a conspiracy which spans three decades. It began in 1972, when President Richard N. Bixion signed an Executive Order that officially started NASA's Space Shuttle Project. He then appointed his nephew Dan Pigeon who had just graduated from Yale University, to head NASA's new Space Shuttle Project. Once settled into his appointed position, Dan recruited a brilliant young computer scientist, who also recently graduated from Yale, for a top position on NASA's new computer design team. That young man was Lee Bradford and the team which Bradford headed only six months after joining NASA, was given the mission of upgrading NASA's entire computer network. This team then built the computer and the program which enabled NASA's computers to create a precise computerized design of the spacecraft, needed for the President's new Space Shuttle Project.

James Aiello

Forbidden Child III Exposed

The upgrades of NASA's computers were completed on September 10, 1973, and work on the computer design for NASA's new Space Shuttle began two days later. NASA records show the computer design for the new spacecraft was completed by the same group of NASA Scientists, headed by Lee Bradford in December of '74. Shortly after, in January of '75, Lee Bradford resigned from NASA and immediately established Bradford Computers Incorporated. Then in June of '75, NASA began awarding contracts to build the new Space Shuttle. That's when Bradford Computers received a twenty year, one hundred billion dollar government contract to build all the computers NASA would need for its Space Shuttle Program; thus, in one day, turning Bradford Computers into the largest computer manufacturer on the face of the earth.

My next astonishing discovery came upon the examination of every aspect of Bradford Computers. For the six years that Bradford Computers held NASA's shuttle account, the company was purchasing all the electrical components for the computers from Westly Electronics. Then I find out Westly Electronics was a front corporation actually owned by Dan Pigeon himself.

Needless to say, both men made a fortune between the years of 1975, and 1981. But that all came to an end the moment Senator Kenney called for a Congressional Investigation. Only their greed didn't stop there, because Bradford and Pigeon were not about to give up their lucrative arrangement that easily. So they had to devise a way around Congress before an investigation could be voted on. Once they decided on a course of action they had vice-president George Rush delay the vote for the 1981 hearing, while Pigeon and Bradford publicly cancelled the contract between NASA and Bradford Computers, stating: 'The fact that Senator Bradford was a former employee of NASA was simply an oversight on NASA's part.'

While this was being done publicly, Lee Bradford, who was the top computer scientist in the field at the time, was secretly slipping into NASA's mainframe through his own private back door. Once in NASA's computers, he planted a virus which would without detection, slowly disable every computer system for the Shuttle Project that was not manufactured by Bradford Computers. His next move was to switch the computer design for the O-rings on the shuttle's solid rocket boosters, with a flawed design. He knew under the right conditions of cold weather during a launch, the flawed O-ring design would fail, allowing hot gasses to leak out of the boosters through the joints. Flames from within the booster would then be able to stream past the failed seals, causing the spacecraft to disintegrate into a ball of fire. From that point on, they sat by watching and waiting, as time after time NASA suffered numerous computer system delays and shutdowns. Then on January 28th, 1986, their waiting ended with the Challenger Disaster.

After the Challenger, all shuttle missions were halted, while a special commission appointed by then, President Feagan determined the cause of the accident. The commission which was also headed by Senator Lee Bradford said, 'NASA's decision to launch the shuttle was flawed, due to an inferior computer monitoring system. The system failed to alert top-level decision-makers, of problems with the joints and O-rings, or the possible damaging effects of cold weather on them both.'

After that Shuttle Designers, with help from Bradford Computers, made several technical modifications, including an improved O-ring design and the addition of a crew bail-out system. The commission's findings then helped justify Dan Pigeon's decision in May of `87, to once again award Bradford Computers the entire shuttle contract. After discovering all this, I realized the only reason George Rush wanted to conceal this crime, was simply to cover his own back. He knew if his vice-presidential choice was caught up in a conspiracy against NASA, it would have crippled his administration before he was even sworn into office.

Now, if you will compare the O-ring design which is dated Jan 15th, 1979, which I received from Lee Bradford in `81, to the design which the Commission **headed by Lee Bradford** submitted to NASA after the Challenger Disaster, you will find they are one and the same. My Fellow Americans, all the evidence I've presented is why I am now publicly accusing Senator Lee Bradford and Former Vice President Dan Pigeon, of the calculated destruction of the Challenger Spacecraft and the cold blooded murder of the Challenger's seven member crew."

From that moment on, we were plunged into a four month nightmare which nearly consumed our every thought, as we were deluged with questions on a daily basis. It was awful! Between the White House, the FBI, the CIA and Congress, I was going nuts. But worst of all were the press, for they were ruthless with their persistent questioning. The world's eyes were on us with such intensity that it was impossible to shield Taylor from the madness. Finally at 2:00pm on November 3rd, 1996, the whole unbelievable ordeal came to an end with the sentencing of Lee Bradford and Dan Pigeon to 'life without parole'. As we made our way from the courthouse to the limo after the sentencing that day, we were swamped by the press and their questions as they shouted, "Christina!   Are you satisfied with the verdict?"

I knew I had to respond to their questions so I stopped and said, "I am pleased with the verdict, but at the same time dismayed with the reality that trusted leaders of our nation could actually perpetrate such a violent act, for the purpose of financial gain."

Then came the next question, "Christina, what are your views of the new Republican Presidential Candidate, Senator Zole?"

I smiled as I replied, "I haven't had the time to see where he stands on the issues as of yet, so I don't feel I'm adequately informed to answer that question fairly."

I pointed for the next question, "Christina, with the election only a few days away, how would you rate the current Administration's accomplishments?"

With a disappointed tone I replied, "I'd feel much more confident in their ability to get things done, if I saw a little less rhetoric and a lot more action.   The fact there is still no Comprehensive National Health Care Program, or how quickly the President folded on the issue of 'Gays in The Military' leaves me disillusioned, to say the least."

The young reporter was swift with his follow-up, "Well, then how do you feel about the independent party's candidate?"

I nearly laughed at that one, but I managed to keep it to a smile as I replied, "The concept of running our nation as a business is just the kind of radical change I believe our nation needs, but I think we should have someone a little more stable to implement such a dramatic overhaul of our government."

"That's quite a controversial statement," the reporter stated.   "Especially since Mr. Proeat has already proven his ability as a successful business man?"

"Maybe so, but you asked for my opinion and I gave it to you."

"Are you saying you could do better?" He quickly replied.

I answered with an air of confidence, "Without a doubt!   Now it's already been a long day so I'll take only one more question."

"Christina, if you can't find one virtue among the field of candidates; then, why don't you consider running for office yourself?"

That's when I started laughing as I answered, "I have enough to do already with raising a four year old, **BUT I'LL THINK ABOUT IT.**"

CHAPTER 10

We thought once the verdict was in we'd go back to our secluded lives, so immediately after that interview we left Washington, D.C., and headed for our home on the Powers Complex in Milton, N.Y. From there our plans were to wait a few weeks for things to cool down, and then sneak back to our mountain hideaway; except once again fate stepped in with her impeccable timing and changed our plans completely.

For you see the day after the trial ended, just happened to be November 4, Election Day 1996. That morning as Jimmy, Michael and I read the papers over breakfast; we were actually amazed by what we read. The front page headlines hardly had anything to do with the election at all. It seemed the whole world was so consumed with the trial, the verdict, and my participation in both, that it became the story everyone wanted to read about. Of course the headlines featured 'little old me' as a national hero, with captions like the New York Times ran, **"Christina Powers topples corrupt government officials with her own style of justice."** It went on to read, **"Then she says she is contemplating running for the White House herself in the year 2000!"** Or like the one the Post ran, **"After exposing the crime of the millennium Christina Powers answers, 'Without a doubt.' when asked if she could do a better job heading our nation than the current Presidential candidates."**

I could see by the look on Michael's face he was not pleased with the headlines insinuating that I may run for President in 2000, but he let it pass without even one comment.

That was until Jimmy looked at me with excitement on his face, in his eyes, and radiating from his voice as he asked, "Christina are you really thinking of running for the White House in 2000?"

"No!" Michael answered sharply. "She has no plans to run for the Presidency. The press took her statement out of context, that's all." Then he looked at me with concern in his eyes and asked me point blank, "You're not really thinking about running are you?"

I answered with a reassuring smile, "No, Michael, I'm not. I have more than enough to do just taking care of you and Taylor, so I sure don't need to add running for President to my list of things to do."

Jimmy obviously didn't sense Michael's irritation to the subject when he popped out with, "But just think Christina. You could be the first woman President of the United States. I know you would make a great President and look at all the opportunities you would have to make life better for all Americans."

Again, Michael answered for me with, "Jimmy, did you or didn't you hear her just say no?"

"Yes, but…" Jimmy tried to answer again.

Michael trying to put an end to the discussion said, "I don't want to hear another word about Christina running for the White House. You got that, Jimmy?"

I think Jimmy got the picture when he snapped 'that wrist' at Michael and said, "Well, you don't have to get nasty about it, Michael. I was only trying to say I think Christina would make a great President, that's all."

"You're right Jimmy, she would be an excellent President, but she's still not running."

At that point the conversation was dropped, but little did we know it wasn't going to be the end of the subject, for later on that morning when we went to our local firehouse in Milton to vote, there was a large banner stretched across the front of the building which read, **"Christina Powers for President in 2000!"**

There was also a large group of reporters just waiting for our arrival, and the first question asked was, "Christina, are you going to run for the Presidency in the year 2000?"

I replied with complete sincerity, "I have no intentions of running for the White House, so I'm afraid there's no story here guys."

We voted, and then headed back to the limo, and on our way home Michael took my hand in his and said, "Punkie, this is starting to concern me. I know you have a way of getting caught up in things, but this is the Presidency of the United States we're talking about. Do you realize how something like this could change our lives forever?"

I kissed his cheek softly and answered, "Yes, honey, I do realize what it would do to our lives and Taylor's. That's why you have my word, I will never run for the White House and I promise you, so please try not to worry about it anymore. All right?"

He kissed my hand and with a sense of relief said, "I'm so glad to hear you say that."

Just then, my cell phone rang and I answered by saying, "Hi, how's Taylor?" Fully expecting to hear Jimmy's voice and instead I heard,

"You go, girlfriend!"

"Barbara, is that you?" I asked, pleasantly surprised.

"Of course it's me, sister." She answered with excitement. "I just heard you're going to run for the White House in 2000, and I want you to know I will back you all the way."

Forbidden Child III Exposed

"Barbara," I tried to interrupt.

"Christina, you know I'm the President of the League of Women Voters and I promise you, I will start a grass roots' movement right now to get your name on the ballot as the Independent Party's nominee for President in 2000."

"But Barbara!" I tried again.

Oh my God, I'm so excited. I can't believe this. It's like a dream come true for me. Christina, I'm flying in tonight so expect me for dinner. We need to talk, because I'm willing to grovel for a position on your cabinet. Like maybe even vice-president."

I finally interrupted by shouting, "Slow down, Barbara! Before you go tallying up the votes you need to know I'm not running for President. I don't know where you heard I was, but it's not true."

"Please don't tell me that," Barbara whined. "I was just about to orgasm, and you go and tell me it's not true."

"Sorry to burst your bubble baby, but there is no way I'm running for the White House."

With a saddened tone she replied, "Can't we even discuss this?"

"There's nothing to discuss Barbara. I don't want to be President. But you're still more than welcomed to come for dinner."

"What? It's been two years since I've seen my nephew; of course I'm still coming for dinner. I should be there around 7:00pm. Oh shit, I have to run, I'm needed back on the set, but we'll talk more when I see you tonight. *Ta ta* for now, girlfriend, love ya."

"Love you too, Barbara."

Throughout my conversation Michael was listening intently, and when I placed the phone in its cradle he turned to me with a painful look on his face and said, "It's starting already, isn't it?"

At first I laughed, but Michael failed to see the humor in it so I smiled confidently and replied, "Barbara wants to be my running mate. Can you believe this? She said she'd love being vice-president, and has invited herself over for dinner this evening to talk to both of us about it."

Michael shook his head, "That's just what I meant, before we know it, everyone and their brother is going to want you to run for President."

I laughed again then said, "It's only Barbara, Michael. You know how radical she is, besides I've already put a stop to it so don't worry."

He kissed me and with a big smile said, "Don't worry, huh! I've heard that before my love, and the more I hear you say it, the more I know there's something to worry about."

Laughing again I said, "You know you're right! Maybe we do have something to worry about."

"Just being married to you is enough to worry about, please don't give me any more grief!" He exclaimed with a smile.

"You should worry, smart ass!" I answered with a sexy wink, "I'm the best thing that's ever happened to you."

He playfully began to tickle me as he said, "You're a pain in the *tuckus,* that's what you are, but you're worth it."

CHAPTER 11

We were laughing like two fools when James pulled the limo up to the front door of our Milton home. As soon as we climbed out of the car, Jimmy came bursting out of the house with Taylor, and with the excitement of a school girl said, "You guys are not going to believe this, but Reverend Jessie Jensen called, and get this, he wants to speak with **you** about possibly joining your campaign! Can you believe it, Jessie Jensen? He's a legend in his own time, and he wants to join your campaign, Christina! Girlfriend, doesn't that tell you something, like maybe you should at least think about it? I took his number and told him I'd have you return his call as soon as you came in, so you need to call him right away Christina, he's waiting!"

I took Taylor out of Jimmy's over excited grasp and said, "You should have just told him it's not true; then, I wouldn't have to call him at all now, would I?"

Then I kissed Taylor and said, "Did you miss us, honey?"

"No Mom, I was playing with Meme." He answered with a smile. Then he cupped his little hands together and whispered in my ear, "Mom, are you going to be the President?"

I kissed his cheek as I chuckled, "No honey, I'm not going to be President."

He gave me one of his heartwarming smiles and said, "That's good Mom, because I don't like it when you have to be away from me."

"Aaa honey, I love you and I don't like being away from you either baby."   I answered lovingly.

"Ha, little man!"   Michael interrupted as he reached for Taylor, "Come over here and give your dad a huge hug."

Without warning Taylor leaped from my arms into Michael's and said, "Don't worry Dad, Mom's not going to be President, I am."

Michael smiled at Taylor and replied, "That's great news, Taylor."   Then he looked at me as he continued, "And Mommy is going to call the reverend right now and tell him that, aren't you mom?"

I kissed both their cheeks and said, "I sure am, guys!"   And off I went.

Reverend Jensen was disappointed that I was not going to run for office, but he handled it gracefully. Barbara on the other hand was far from graceful.

She started in on us immediately after dinner that evening and when Michael and I outright refused to even discuss my running for office with her, she slapped her hand down on the table, and with frustration in her voice said, "Why are you both being so damned obstinate? Can't you see you're the perfect candidate?   Please guys, just listen to me for one minute, if not for your own sake, then Taylor's.   Christina, our world is in deep shit as we head into the twenty first century.   If we don't do something drastic to change things right now while we still have time; then, we might as well light a match to the dreams of our children. The earth won't last other hundred-years, if the human race continues the course that we're on."

"Ouch!"   I said interrupting.   "That was below the belt."

"You left me no choice, but to be blunt."   She

replied firmly. "How else can I make you see how desperate the situation really is?"

"We know things aren't perfect in the world Barbara," Michael interrupted. "But that doesn't mean Christina has got to run for President in order to make a difference."

Just then Taylor sat up and said, "Aunt Barbara, why do you think the world won't last a hundred more years?"

Barbara smiled gently at Taylor, "That's a very good question, honey. The reason I'm so concerned is because the human race as a whole is polluting our planet so much, scientists believe if we don't begin to take care of the earth and stop polluting it; then, the earth will no longer be able to sustain human life for another hundred years."

At that point I got up from my seat, "I think we've heard enough on this topic for tonight, besides it's Taylor's bedtime." Glancing over to Michael I continued, "Why don't you take everyone to the family room and check on the election results, while I get Taylor ready for bed."

He agreed and once Taylor completed his round of hugs and kisses we headed up for bed.

CHAPTER 12

Taylor was unusually quiet during his bath that evening, and every time I'd ask if there was something bothering him, he would slap my arm forcefully and say, "Just stop talking, Mom!"

After the third slap, I figured I'd better stop talking before my arm turned black and blue. I knew what he was upset over and I wanted to comfort him, but I also knew I couldn't force him to talk about it either. So after his bath, I tried small talk, "How was your dinner, honey?" For my efforts I received another slap.

"I said stop talking, Mom!"

"Hey, what do you think I am your punching bag?" I caught the hint of a smile, so while he was trying to put on his PJ's, I tried a little tickling.

He pushed me away and said, "Please stop, Mom," with such intensity I nearly started to cry for him right on the spot.

I dropped my hands and said, "Aaa! I'm sorry, honey.   I promise I'll stop talking right now."

I said nothing more until he gave me a strange look and shouted, "Well, are you going to read my story tonight or do I have to do that for you too." I fought back my laughter and immediately started reading chapter six of, **The Lion, The Witch and the Wardrobe**.

After story time was over, Taylor looked up at

me with sad eyes, quickly wrapped his precious little arms around my neck and said, "I love you, Mom." Then he laid his head on my breast and in a soft gentle tone asked, "Mom, what is pollution?"

Feeling relieved he was finally opening up, I smiled and lovingly answered, "Pollution is a foreign substance which can cause something clean like drinking water, to become impure and unsafe to drink. It's usually a by-product of mankind's own ingenuity, which simply means we create pollution ourselves."

Still wearing a sad face he again gazed into my eyes, and with a confused tone said, "I don't understand, Mom. If pollution is really hurting the earth like Aunt Barbara says it is, then why does everyone continue to make pollution?"

I held him tenderly as I tried to answer my four year old's seemingly innocent question, "It's a little complicated honey, and I don't know all the answers myself, but I'll try to explain it. I think the biggest reason is because as individual nations, we really don't know how to live and compete in an industrialized world economy, without causing pollutants."

He looked up at me with the expression of a little genius brainstorming and enthusiastically said, "I got it, Mom. All we have to do is learn how to stop polluting ourselves; then, we can teach everyone else how."

I hugged and kissed him, then said, "That's a brilliant idea honey, and we can start working on the problem first thing in the morning if you'd like, but right now we need to say our prayers so you can get some sleep."

He kissed me, then we both knelt beside his bed and he said, "Dear God, please bless Mommy, Daddy, Nanny, Meme and the whole world. And please help Mom and me learn how to stop polluting, so we can

Forbidden Child III Exposed

teach everyone else. I love you God, and please bless Baby Jesus, too.   Amen."

I kissed his forehead as I tucked him into bed and said, "Goodnight sweetheart, and have only pleasant dreams my love."   Then, I began to softly sing a lullaby and as I watched my little angel drift off to sleep, I found myself feeling totally humbled by the innocence of this wondrous child's uncorrupted intelligence.

Forbidden Child III Exposed

CHAPTER 13

Later on when I entered the living room everyone was glued to the TV as Dan Rather was tallying up the final numbers for the 1996 Presidential Vote.

I quietly took a seat beside Michael and said, "Try to remind me later and I'll tell you what he said, he was so cute tonight."

Michael, smiled as he replied, "Isn't he always?"

I nodded my head in agreement and asked, "Who's winning?"

"Dan's about to tell us now."   Barbara answered, as she turned up the volume on the TV's remote to hear Dan, say, "With all the votes in, it now appears that with 52% of the vote, Democratic President, Bill Baxter, will be staying in the White House for another four years.   I have a special note here tonight.   During our CBS voter poll we discovered that if Christina Powers had been in the race for the White House this evening, she would have swept the election with a whopping 68% of the vote.   Now that's a statistic I'm sure both political Party's are going to have to take notice of."

Just then Barbara clicked off the set, turned to Michael and me, and said, "I told you!   For God sakes Michael, please talk some sense into this girl."

Michael shook his head and said, "Don't think I'm going to help you Barbara, I don't want her running for President any more than she does."

Barbara sighed in frustration as she said, "Can't you guys see how serious the world crisis really is right now?   Dammit guys, the human race is hurdling toward self-destruction and no one is really even willing to admit it, no less make the hard decisions which need to be made in order to solve the problem.   I'm telling both of you that if people like us, who have been given so much in this lifetime don't do something to stop the destruction of the human race; then, no one will, and one day it will all go up in flames."

With my own frustration I asked, "Well if you're so sure things are all that bad, then why don't you run for President yourself?"

Her eyes lit up as she replied, "I would in a heartbeat if I thought I could win, but even as popular with the public as I am, my name doesn't carry the clout yours does girlfriend.   Christina, the majority of Americans love and trust you, they've seen you in action and they know what you've accomplished.   They also know you're respected and feared by the world's leaders and that's something even our current President can't claim.   These are just some of the reasons why you would make a great President.   Christina, our nation needs the kind of strong leadership skills you alone possess."

"Barbara, please stop."   I interrupted. "I'm not running for President and that's final, but I will try to become more active in social programs, and I will be more vocal on environmental issues.   This I promise!" On that note, we ended the conversation.

I've always called for strict environmental controls on all my corporate holdings.   But the next morning before I even served breakfast, I discovered that Taylor was determined to see just how well Powers Incorporated held up to his pollution test.   By the end of the day, we had gathered all the statistics needed to make a fair judgment on the clean-up performance of Power's

Incorporated, and according to Taylor, we failed miserably, even though we led the world's industries in environmental improvements.

His answer to the accomplishments of our overall improvements in reducing pollutants was, "We have to figure out how to stop all polluting right now Mom, or it's still going to kill our planet."

Once again I was amazed by his intellect and all I could say was, "You're right honey, we do."

In response to my answer, he looked at Michael and I as he raised his hands to his cheeks and said, "How are we going to figure this one out, guy's?"

We all started to laugh and I answered, "I don't know honey, but I guess it's one we'll all have to figure out together, won't we?"

From that day on Michael and I set all the brawn and brains of Powers Incorporated into coming up with answers to our pollution questions. I wanted documented proof of all known pollutants, their causes and their effects on our environment. I also wanted solid solutions on how to stop the pollutants and reverse their environmental damage. For the next two months while we were diving head-first into the environmental issues, we were also besieged by every special interest group across the nation, all wanting to support my candidacy for President. I continued to gracefully decline all the support and after a while the clamor began to subside.

Finally on March 1st, 1997, we were able to quietly sneak back to our mountain hideaway. With us we had six large boxes of pollution statistics to study. Michael and I studied those statistics for the next two weeks with Taylor looking over our shoulders the entire time. And the more we learned the clearer it became to the three of us that Barbara was right, we're in deep shit!

Forbidden Child III Exposed

For the next few days we thought about what we had learned so far. The true facts were so overwhelming we didn't know what to do, but no matter what steps we took, running for President was not going to be one of them. Or so we thought. But the events which took place on March 16th, 1997 had the power to change the course of our futures forever.

That morning began with Michael and me lying in bed openly discussing our findings, when Taylor surprised us by entering our room unannounced. Then, he slowly began to walk toward us wearing a saddened expression on his face. When he reached the bed he said, "It doesn't sound like there's much chance of solving this one, guys."

Michael, snatched him up into his arms and said, "Don't look so down little Punkie, there's plenty we can do."

"That's right," I added as I began to tickle him. "You just watch your Mom and Dad in action." With that, Taylor leaped into my arms and shouted, "I'm glad to hear that, Mom. I just learned to do a handstand and Meme said if I practice; I could be in the Olympics someday." Then, he jumped off the bed and shouted again, "Watch me, guys!"

As we watched our little monkey laughing and playing, 'confident' that his parents would solve the world's problems, we knew somehow we had to make the peoples of the world see just how contaminated our planet really is. Then, maybe together humanity could make the changes needed to save the future for our children; a future, I only just discovered would be riddled with toxic death from all corners of the globe, if we don't begin to act now.

After breakfast that morning, the three of us headed into the office to brainstorm with my top environmental people.   I wanted to know all the options to determine the best way to proceed with our mission to clean up the earth, before going public.

Just as our meeting began, Pierre came to me and handed me a note which read, **"Christina, President Baxter is on the line for you."**

Looking at him strangely I thought, "The President, what could he want?"   Then I thanked him, excused myself for a moment and headed to my office to take the call in private.

When I reached my desk, I picked up the phone and with a tone of curiosity said, "Hello, Mr. President. This is Christina Powers.   How can I help you?"

"Please Christina, call me Bill."   He replied in a casual tone, "I've known you for so long, I feel as though we're old friends."

"Well thank you Bill, that's very kind of you."   I answered with sincerity.

"Christina, forgive me for taking you from your meeting, but this call is more of a personal matter concerning a dear friend of yours.   We thought it best for you to hear this directly from him yourself.   As we speak, I'm also connected via a satellite to Saudi Arabia. Mohammed, are you able to hear Christina?"

"Yes, Mr. President quite well," replied a voice I recognized instantly.   "And I thank you for your assistance."

"You're welcome," Bill answered.   "Now I'll get off the line so you may break the news to Christina in private."

With that the President hung up and left me to speak with someone I knew to be a mad man.

"Good morning, Christina my friend," he began very properly.   "This is your 'brother in spirit,' Mohammed Fehd.   My call is to inform you personally of the deeply sad event which has taken place this very night in the Holy City of Mecca. My father, King Toudia Fehd has passed over to great Allah in the Seventh Heaven."

"I'm sorry to hear of your loss Mohammed," I facetiously remarked, "But why would you think I would want to hear this news from you personally?"

With a sincere tone he answered, "I would think you would, because I still believe we are two spirits with one destiny, my sister. And I wanted you to know of my father's passing before I tell my people and the world."

"Well, soon to be King," I replied sarcastically. "I thank you for this revelation, but neither your father's passing, nor your taking his throne, has any interest to me at all. So I'm afraid you've wasted a call. Now I'm very busy, so I really must say goodbye."

"Please Christina, don't be so hasty! I haven't called to harass you. I guess I deserved that after the way I behaved at our last meeting, but I was hoping we could be civil enough to put that all behind us. I need you to know Christina that I've learned much from watching your life unfold over the years, and it has changed the way I'm looking at the world these days. I just wanted you to know when I take the throne of the wealthiest nation on earth; I will be dedicating the address I've written to my nation and the world, to you, Christina Powers."

I was taken aback by his statement, so I interrupted by saying, "Let me see if I understand this, Mohammed. I think you're trying to tell me I've made some kind of a positive impact on the way you're looking at life these days? I find that hard to believe."

He chuckled with a tone of sophistication then said, "More than just a positive look my friend! You have helped me to reach the true power of my own divinity, when you gave birth to your little miracle, and I want to share this knowledge with the world as you do. This is why I think you will find my address this evening very interesting."

Relaxing my sarcasm somewhat I said, "I'm still not sure I understand the message behind this call Mohammed, but I will try to watch your address just the same. If nothing else, you've at least peaked my curiosity."

"That's wonderful." He roared with enthusiasm. "CNN will be airing my address live to the world in the morning. You should be able to view the broadcast on your local station at 8:00pm your time this evening. I'm sure you and your family will find what I have to say very enlightening."

"I will be watching Mohammed, now I really must say goodbye."

"So must I my sister, for my destiny is beckoning. Now I wish you well till we meet again, Christina."

After that call I took Michael aside and filled him in on my conversation with Mohammed. As soon as I finished speaking Michael looked at me with a confused expression and said, "What do you think this is all about?"

I shook my head and answered, "I haven't got a clue honey, and I'm not going to worry about figuring it out either. Besides, I'm sure we'll know more by the time he finishes his address and we'll deal with it then. We have real things to deal with right now, just ask Taylor."

Michael smiled as he replied, "You're right and if we don't get back to work soon, we're going to hear about it." With that we shrugged Mohammed off.

CHAPTER 14

The rest of that day, I went through the motions like any other day, acting as if I was in control of everything, but in reality I couldn't have felt more helpless than if I were a little girl lost in the wilderness. All I could think about was my conversation with Mohammed and how frightened I really was of this man. Finally the day ended and it was time to head home. Since I was concerned over what we might be hearing that evening, I asked Jimmy to come spend the night with Taylor, so Michael and I could watch Mohammed's address without Taylor's presence. Jimmy agreed, and when we arrived home I quickly served dinner then sent Taylor and Jimmy off to play in Taylor's room, while Michael and I got ready to watch CNN.

8:00pm came slower than I thought it should, but when it finally arrived we found ourselves glued to the TV set the moment Mohammed took center stage. His appearance on the TV was awesome. He glistened like an angel in all his kingly attire, and he moved with such majesty as he took his place on his father's throne, that he resembled a god incarnate.

As I watched him take his place I thought with a chuckle, "I should have taken him out when I had the chance."

Once Mohammed was settled he began his address by mourning the loss of his father, then by touting the former King's achievements over his lifetime. After a more than honorable eulogy to his father's memory, he spoke of his father's dreams for his nation.

Then he said, "Now as I take my place as king of our great nation, I know I have much to do if I want to see my father's dreams for our people come true. This is why I thank Allah. This is a Godly people I am commissioned to lead into the future, and we must never forget the great strides our beloved king has made for our nation and her people. We must also never forget King Toudia's desire to achieve total peace in the Middle East. And not just for Saudi Arabia, but for all the rest of the Middle East as well. Because of my father's dream I find myself determined to lead Palestine along with all her Arab brothers, into a true peace with the Jewish state of Israel."

He began to remove the crown of gold from his head as he rose from his throne. Then he knelt down and as he placed his crown on the floor he said, "I do this as a symbolic jester to show all men I am their equal." Then he rose to a standing position and continued, "Words of great wisdom which have come from a woman I have learned to honor and respect, have only recently helped me to believe that such a peace as my father dreamed of for the Middle East, is truly possible. The woman I speak of is known to the world as the 'Angel of Peace,' and that woman is my sister in spirit, Christina Powers. Christina, I'd like to thank you right now for the great lesson of unconditional love you have taught me. Without your insight in the ways of the Almighty, I may have never realized that the power of Allah's love resides within us all. For as Christina has said, it is time to stop passing judgment on our fellow man, and start loving them for the good that is innately instilled within all of us, instead of hanging onto all the hate and bigotry of a time that's best forgotten. This is why I will be inviting the leaders of Israel and Palestine to meet with me in the Holy City of Mecca, to discuss and hopefully sign an everlasting Peace Accord. A Peace Accord that will begin a new legacy of love between the Arabs and Jews, which I know will have the power to conquer the legacy of hatred left to us by our forefathers."

Michael and I looked at each other with stunned expressions as he spoke. We actually found ourselves speechless by what we were hearing. And much to our surprise Mohammed was only beginning to blow us away, for his next sentence was, "It is time for Arabs and Jews to look past the hatred taught to us in the Bible and the Koran, and begin looking toward a peaceful future. For once we can move beyond the doctrine of hatred; we will be able to see we are all equal in the eyes of God, whose eyes are yours and mine. Now to show to Israel and the world, that the Arab people mean what we say, I will list just a few of the proposals I will bring to the peace talks with Israel. First, Saudi Arabia will promise to pay twenty billion dollars in Western currency, to the government of Israel to relinquish the occupied territories in the West Bank and the Gaza Strip, to the Nation of Palestine. Second, we will pledge another twenty billion dollars in Western currency to the government of Palestine, along with economic advisors to help establish Palestine, as a viable democratic nation. Third, I will ask the people of Palestine to relinquish all their historical claims to the Holy City of Jerusalem, and honor the right of the Nation of Israel to keep Jerusalem as their Capital City. In turn, I will request that Israel freely open the doors of the City of Jerusalem to the unimpeded movement of all Arabs in a city which the Arab World also reveres as Holy. Fourth, if a peace accord is signed as I believe it will be, then Saudi Arabia will remove the Islamic Temple and also pledge as a gift to the people of Israel, another twenty billion dollars to rebuild the temple of David to its original glory, and on the original site King David had it built over six thousand years ago. Fifth, I will personally pledge to work hand-in-hand with the Nation of Israel, until its leaders have signed peace accords with all the nations of my Arab brothers. Sixth, I know in order to finance the peace I hope for in the Middle East, Saudi Arabia will have to pull large amounts of cash reserves from the banks of Western Nations, as well as, liquidate most of our holdings in these nations. Because of this I also pledge to help offset any harmful effects to the economies of the West, by purchasing all the needed supplies from these Western Nations to rebuild the nations of the Arab world. Then one day all of my Arab brother nations will become thriving members of the world community. As I have said, these are only a few of the proposals I will bring to peace talks with Israel, and I'm hopeful that these along with the rest of my proposals, will help us all to finally realize a true peace for the Middle East in our lifetime. The legacy I want to leave my five year old son is one of peace and life, not hatred and death. I now want to thank all of you for taking time to hear my ideas on how to establish world peace, and I pray Allah may bless the futures of us all."

The moment the commercial came on I clicked off the set, turned to Michael, and with complete exuberance said, "I can't believe this!   This is wonderful news, Michael. Do you realize what he just did? He paved the way for real peace in the Middle East, and he thanked me for planting the seeds of peace in his heart. This is too good to be true."

Michael motioned with his hands for me to lower

my voice as he said, "Calm down before you have Taylor in here."

I lowered my voice to say, "I'm sorry honey, I'm just so excited."

Michael hugged me joyfully and said, "Why don't we go outside to discuss this, before we end up having to explain to Taylor why his Mom's bouncing off the walls."

I playfully kissed his cheek several times then said, "Good idea, handsome. I'll go get our coats while you let Jimmy and Taylor know were going for a walk."

He patted my buns as I turned from him and said, "Hurry back ya little screwball."

We strolled arm in arm along the mountain roads that evening, and in our hearts we felt a new sense of hope for Taylor's future.

As we walked, I lovingly squeezed Michael's arm and said, "Michael, I feel so pleased with myself that something I've said or done has caused such a remarkable change in that man's life, and I truly believe he has the ability to accomplish what he's set out to do."

"It's something to be proud of Punkie. You've helped to create the largest movement toward peace on earth the human race has ever known. Now, all we have to do is get him to join us with cleaning up the planet, and we'll be set."

With that statement I stopped walking, hugged Michael with enthusiasm and said, "That's a fabulous thought Michael, and I'll bet we can get him to help us too!"

Just then Michael shouted with excitement as he pointed toward the northwestern sky, "Look, Christina! I think we're seeing the first visible sighting to the naked eye of Comet Hal-Bop. Isn't it beautiful?"

I gazed in the direction of the comet and with a

sense of awe said, "Oh my God!   It's breathtaking, Michael."

We found ourselves captivated by the wonder of the comet, and with my eyes still fixed on this awesome sight I said, "I wonder if the Star of David shone with such splendor when it lit up the skies over Bethlehem. Do you realize it was nearly two thousand years ago, when that star brought the good news of the birth of Christ?"

Michael turned to me and in a purely spiritual way said, "Isn't it appropriate that this comet should appear over the earth on the same evening King Mohammed would announce his plans to rebuild the Temple of David."

In a flash, icicles shot up my spine, as echoes of a vow once made to me came rushing to my consciousness. "Remember this, Christina Powers! I will be standing as the divine ruler in the Temple of David when I have you beheaded."

Fear shot the words from my mouth as I shouted, "Oh my God! Michael! He's using his wealth and power to manipulate the world in the name of peace, and he's doing it all just to gain his own ultimate evil goals." With horror radiating from my eyes, I looked at Michael and continued, "Michael, his true goal is to annihilate the Jewish race from the face of the earth, and rule the world from his throne in the Holy City of Jerusalem."

"Wow!   Slow down!"   Michael strongly protested, "If that were true, why would he thank you for opening his heart to peace?"

I looked at Michael as if he were stupid and said, "Can't you see the bastard is trying to use the world's faith in my reputation to gain their trust in him. Michael don't you remember the vow he made to me concerning the Temple of David?"

Forbidden Child III Exposed

Michael's face instantly turned white and when he caught his breath he said, "Holy shit! Do you really think he's capable of accomplishing his goals?"

I shook my head and answered, "He most likely has the secret backing of the entire Arab world. I definitely think it's a possibility."

Just then Michael gazed back toward the heavens and in a curious tone said, "I still don't understand how he could hope to conquer the world. Especially if he's giving most of his wealth to Israel."

I thought for a moment as I joined Michael in gazing up at the stars and replied, "Sixty billion dollars is nothing to a man like that. He has vast holdings all over the world, especially in the United States." Then it hit me! I grabbed Michael's arm with brute force and excitedly said, "That's it, Michael; he plans to slowly undermine the economies of the west by transferring his financial and industrial holdings throughout the world to the Arab Nations. All he has to do is get the ball rolling in the name of peace, and the West will be unwittingly sucked into his plans without revolting once. I'll bet the moment he sends the economies of the world into a nose dive; he'll be attacking Israel from within her own borders. The only thing I can't figure out is whether he's hoping I don't figure this out, so he can use me in his plans, or if he's openly challenging me to a sick chess game with the world's nations' as our pawns!"

This time Michael had the look of fear as he said, "Is there any way we can stop him?"

I shook my head in bewilderment and replied, "I don't know, Michael. I just don't know."

I truly believed Michael and I prayed for guidance that night harder then we'd ever prayed for anything in our entire lives. We were both frightened by the future we saw unfolding for humanity, and the foresight we held of things to come only broke our hearts. We knew if nothing was done right now to change the course the human race was on, then there would be no future for any of our children. Needless to say, with the apprehension we felt that night neither one of us slept too well.

The next morning as we surfed the web we knew our fears were well founded. The front pages of the newspapers across the globe all shouted the praises of King Mohammed Fehd to the entire world, with headlines like the one the London Times ran, **"Saudi Arabia declares King Mohammed Fehd their 'King of Peace' as he takes the throne of the wealthiest nation on earth!"** Better yet, listen to the one the New York Post ran, **"King Fehd, the first man to be called the 'King of Peace' since Christ himself!"**

After reading these headlines I turned to Michael, and with disgust in my voice said, "He's a devil in sheep's clothing, just waiting to pounce. He's good too. He disguised himself as the perfect King of Peace last night and that was just his first address to a world audience. I've learned enough about the male psyche to know if you give a man like that time unchecked, he'll slit your throat from behind the first chance he gets."

I think in that moment, Michael realized the situation we found ourselves in was more urgent, then our dreams for the quiet life ever could be. Because the minute I finished talking, he looked at me with anger in his eyes and said, "We have no choice, Christina. For Taylor's sake we have to stop him."

I gently ran my fingers through his hair and with a mischievous look in my eyes replied, "I know we do Michael, and we will."

His angry expressions turned wild as he asked with an aggressive tone, "What do you have in mind, hired assassins?"

I started to laugh then said, "Michael, that's the problem with the typical male response to a perceived threat, you guys always think violence is the answer. What do you want, a murder on our hands? Besides, there's not a hired assassin in the world that would even get close to him, no less kill him. The only way we can stop him is to beat him at his own game."

Michael's wide expression took on a nervous one as he asked, "So how do we do that?"

I looked at him lovingly, realizing he really didn't know the answer and said, "There are three things we need to accomplish if we even hope to have any chance of beating him. First, we're going to have to triple this year's expected earnings for Powers Incorporated, and send our stocks through the roof. We have to be more than just financially sound in order to take up some of the slack when he starts pulling the rug out from under our nation's financial feet. And the only way we're going to accomplish that, is if I go back to work and work harder than I've ever worked in my life. Second, I have to make him believe he's pulled the 'wool over my eyes' as well. Then, maybe I can undermine some of the popularity he holds with his nation's citizens by hitting him where he's most vulnerable."

Michael looked at me as if he really didn't want to know the answer to the question he was about to ask, "What's the third thing?"

I shook my head sadly and said, "I'll have to become President of the United States." I can't even describe Michael's expression. You had to be there.

CHAPTER 15

After breakfast that morning we gave complete charge of Meme, to Taylor, if you know what I mean. Then Michael and I spent the rest of the morning discussing exactly how I felt we should proceed with our mission to get King Mohammed Fehd, before he gets us. As serious as the plotting was, it still only took us till just before lunch to agree on our course of action. Before our lunch break with the kids, I called up our attorney Tom Davies and security Chief Frank Rossi to ask them to come for dinner that evening. We wanted to tell Jimmy, Pierre, Frank and Tom, of our plans as soon as possible, because we knew we were going to need their assistance and right away! We also wanted them to be the only other people on the face of the earth to know what the world would soon be facing from King Fehd, and what we planned to do to stop him.

We said nothing about our decisions to Taylor until just before bedtime prayers that evening. The three of us were sitting on the edge of his bed when Michael looked at Taylor very seriously and said, "Taylor, my boy, your Mom and I need to discuss something with you."

Taylor gazed lovingly into his Dad's eyes and with the happiest little voice said, "Meme and I knew you and Mom were figuring out how to clean up our planet Dad, that's why we didn't disturb you guys when you were working."

We both laughed as we kissed his cheeks, then Michael continued, "You guys were right and that's why we need to talk. Taylor, your Mom and I have learned in order for us to try and clean up the environment, we both have to go back to work."

"What about me?" Taylor interrupted with wide eyes. "What can I do to help?"

I smiled as I answered, "Well honey, you're going to get to come with us. I'm going to put you and Meme in charge of figuring out how to let the children of the world know what to do to help clean up our environment. Your Dad and I have also decided to let you appear in a film with me. What do you think about that?"

His face gleamed as he replied, "Wow! When do we get started?"

I wrapped my arms around him proudly and answered, "Tomorrow morning my little man, but there is still one more thing we need to talk about."

He looked at me curiously and said, "You look sad Mom, what is it?"

I smiled softly, "Honey, going back to work and letting everyone know we're in an environmental mess will help, but if we really want to make changes; then, your Mom will have to run for President."

His expression seemed to glisten as he smiled and answered, "I know Mom, the golden lady in my dream last night already told me you would run for President, and I'm happy because she said Dad and I are going to help you."

I was amazed by his reply, so I kissed his cheek and said, "I'm glad you're happy honey, now I want us to keep this a secret among just the three of us until the time is right. Okay?"

Forbidden Child III Exposed

"All right, Mom," he answered joyfully.

I kissed him again, "I love you, Punkie Doodle. Now let's say our prayers and get some sleep, we have a busy day tomorrow." After he said his prayers we tucked him in and headed back down to Jimmy, Pierre, Frank and Tom. It was time to do some recruiting.

The six of us spent the rest of that evening intensely planning each step we would have to take to reach our goal. Tom's mission was to find every holding King Fehd and his possible allies held throughout the world, and to do research on every move all of the Arab nations made politically and economically over the last ten years, and from now on. And just for curiosity's sake we decided to check out China too. We needed to know just who else was in on Mohammed's plot, and how they might be secretly maneuvering together to collapse the economies of the west. Frank's mission was first to guard Taylor with his life whenever Michael or I couldn't and to increase our security force into the size of a small army. I put Jimmy and Taylor on a project to come up with the best way to help the children of the world become more aware of our current environmental problems. At the same time, teach the things they can do individually and collectively to help stop the destruction of our world. Pierre was to mind our little empire. As for Michael and me, well, we had some money to make and fast.

After our discussions, I decided to call Mohammed on his private line. I placed the call on the speaker phone so everyone could listen in.

The moment Mohammed was on the line I began our conversation with excitement in my voice as I said, "Mohammed, its Christina. I'm calling to thank you for your kind words, and to let you know your speech has touched my heart in a way I never thought possible.

Forbidden Child III Exposed

The things you said brought tears to my eyes, and I want you to know I'm more than honored, that you thanked me for helping to open up your heart to forgiveness and unconditional love."   I then changed my tone to one of true sincerity and added, "My only regret Mohammed is that you didn't understand my heart when there was a chance for us to be a couple."

His voice actually sounded sad as he replied, "I also hold that regret in my heart Christina, for I realized with the remarkable birth of your son, it was you who was meant to be my bride and bear my son. I've asked myself time and time again why we're not together or why I was kept so blind, for so long. But then I think, who am I to question the wisdom of Allah?"

"I don't know the answers either Mohammed." I answered sympathetically.   "What I do know is you've finally found your way into my heart, and if there is anything I can do to help you achieve the peace you and I both dream of, please don't hesitate to call me."

His reply seemed almost genuine, "I will be addressing the U.N. assembly next February, Christina, and I would cut off my left hand just to have dinner with you once more."

I chuckled a little seductively, and then said, "I'm flattered Mohammed, but that's not necessary because I would love to have dinner with you."

We ended our conversation by setting a date for dinner for February 28th, 1998. When I hug-up the phone, Michael turned to me looking very irritated, and with a slightly jealous tone said, "I know you had to sound convincing, but did you have to sound so damned sensual too?"

Jimmy and I started to chuckle at Michael's response, then I tenderly kissed his cheek and said, "Don't get jealous on me now Michael, because I'm going to need to use every trick in the book against this character, if we even hope to have a chance of beating him. And getting him to believe he has a chance with me has got to be my first angle."

Tom spoke up, "Christina, are you sure this guy is really trying to deceive the world?   He sounded pretty sincere to me."

"I was thinking the same thing," Frank added.

"So was I," Michael joined in.

I looked at them all with an unbelieving expression and said, "Have you guys ever seen me scheming this hard for nothing? Besides, all he has to do is come up clean when we start digging, and we'll back right off."   Then, I lifted my eyebrows in a discerning way and continued, "So are you guys, with me, or not?"

They answered simultaneously, "Of course we're with, you!"

I smiled confidently and replied, "That's good, because I don't think I'm wrong about Mohammed's true motives. Now I think we'd better get some rest, there's a lot to do tomorrow."

The first thing we did the following morning, March 18th, 1997, was to dive headfirst into our assignments. Three months later we were preparing to release my first film in over fifteen years. I entitled the film, 'The Slaying of the American Knights.'   The story was about a single mother who worked for the Governor of New York State. The thrills began ten minutes into the film when the heroin, 'yours-truly', stumbles upon a conspiracy between the Governor and three high ranking state officials, to conceal how they knowingly allowed the state's largest chemical and plastics manufacturer, to dump millions of supposedly leak proof barrels of toxic waste into the Hudson River. The barrels that lined the bottom of the river from the mouth of New York harbor to the Port of Albany were slowly leaking toxic death to the entire state. From there the story unfolds with her secret search for proof of what she knows and what she goes through to bring that proof to light. The film had just enough action, drama, love, and suspense to be a major blockbuster, and with Taylor as my little co-star, I knew it couldn't fail.

Released with the film was a ten cut soundtrack entitled, "Follow Me to Utopia." The title cut was a ballad which invited the whole world to follow me as one family into a loving, free, and unpolluted future. The second cut was a souped-up contemporary dance hit entitled, "Self-annihilation." It told how through great hatred, bigotry, and pollution we were destroying ourselves and our earth. It also allowed me to show the world that even at forty three, I was still the queen of the dance floor.

My little co-star and I began promoting our new film with zeal before the editing was even completed. We started by appearing on every talk show in the country, and like magic, Taylor stole the hearts of the nation.

When we appeared on the nation's leading talk show, Taylor immediately stole the spotlight with his big smile as he looked at me and enthusiastically said, "Wow, Mom! We're really on the Opraho Gunthry Show."

The audience immediately began to laugh and after we discussed the film, Opraho looked at Taylor and asked, "So tell us Taylor, did you like making a movie with your Mother?"

He smiled again and replied, "It was great, but the best thing is that my Mom made the movie because I asked her to."

Opraho smiled at him curiously and with a

Forbidden Child III Exposed

surprised tone said, "You did!   Why did you do that?"

Still smiling Taylor answered, "The reason the film is plotted around an environmental disaster is because I asked my Mom and Dad if there was anything the three of us could do to help save our planet.   They told me the only way we could make a difference was to get involved, and the film is one way we're trying to do that.   My Mom, Dad, Uncle Meme, Nana, and all our friends have become members of Green Peace and The Save the Earth Brigade.   I'm also working to establish a worldwide environmental awareness television network, which will be geared toward a younger audience."

It was apparent Opraho was taken aback by Taylor's intellect when she took a deep breath and said, "My goodness!   Wouldn't you rather be playing at the park like most four year old children do?"

Taylor looked at her sadly as he hugged my arm and answered, "Mom, Dad, and I use to play all the time and I miss that, but we know if we don't do something to stop the pollution today, then there won't be a world for anyone to play in tomorrow."   With that Taylor received his first standing ovation.   He got his second two days later on the Josie O'Harra Show.

CHAPTER 16

The film was ready to go on June 3rd, which was calling it close, because we had already arranged to premiere the soundtrack along with clips from the film on June 5th, with a Thursday night blowout concert extravaganza in L.A., and it was being broadcast live on CBS. We premiered the film in New York on Taylor's fifth birthday Saturday, June 7, 1997. Afterward, with a birthday cake and presents, we turned the film's premiere into a city wide birthday party for our Taylor. The first weekend out the film grossed a-record ninety two million dollars nationwide and sales of the soundtrack were beginning to soar. Our success was so phenomenal that by July 1st, we were grossing billions in the world market, our stocks were sky rocketing, and to top it all off I began a five month fifty city concert tour. My popularity was so high; I filled stadiums to capacity as we worked five cities a week, two concerts a night. And with each performance, I would set aside twenty minutes to have an open conversation with the audience about our environmental crises.

The concert tour ended on December 8th, 1997, and in only nine months we had more than reached our financial goals for that year with whopping corporate earnings of two hundred and sixty nine billion dollars.

The time flew by so fast that before we knew it, it was February 28th, 1998, and I found myself reluctantly

Forbidden Child III Exposed

leaving a very nervous Michael behind, as I left for my rendezvous with King Mohammed Fehd at the Saudi Embassy in downtown Manhattan. While heading toward the city that night, I found myself feeling frustrated and uncertain over following through with my mission of international espionage, and sabotage, because with all the information Tom had gathered over the last eleven months, we still had no solid proof Mohammed was doing anything underhanded at all. I guess it was simply pure gut instinct, which compelled me to launch that orchestrated evening of adulterated deception.

The moment James drove the limo through the heavily guarded gates and into the courtyard of the Saudi Embassy, a cold chill of fear came over me and I thought, "Lord Jesus, please give me strength, because I'm really scared, and the last thing I want to be doing right now is looking this guy straight in the eye to try to convince him that I even like him, no less love him."

Just then James pulled the limo to an abrupt stop right in front of the embassy, and the moment one of the armed guards opened my door, I swallowed hard, and immediately became Christina Powers, the most seductive woman on the face of the earth.

Of course, I exited the limo with my right leg first, allowing just enough flesh to show through the slit of my turquoise gown, to heat the frigid February temperature at least 20 degrees. Then to fan the flames, I very slowly and provocatively emerged from the limo radiating sensuality with my every move.

I was not at all surprised to see the King standing at the curb looking better then Ohmar Charieff could have ever hoped to look. The second we made eye contact I gave him one of my famous winks. With that, pure passion flared up from the depths of his dark blue eyes, to the rising bulge in his pants, and instantly I knew I could handle King Mohammed Fehd.

Once I reached him, I slightly curtseyed then very femininely offered him my hand, which he appropriately kissed then released as he passionately said, "Christina, my love, you're more captivating at this moment; then, the most enchanted angel in the heavens, and I must admit that by merely standing in your presence, I'm finding myself actually feeling humbled by just a glance of your wondrously bewitching beauty."

I smiled graciously and seductively replied, "It is a pleasure seeing you again your majesty, and I thank you for your charming flattery, and it was quite the compliment."

He smiled adoringly as he reclaimed my hand and warmly said, "I feel as though I've waited a lifetime for this evening, so won't you please allow me to escort you to the dining room?"

Still smiling I gently squeezed his hand and replied, "I wouldn't want it any other way."

Mohammed poured on the charm as he romantically lead me arm-in-arm through the embassy, and as we spoke with voices of mutual admiration, visions of almost being thrown off a roof by this man began flashing through my mind and I thought, "Oh shit! You better keep your cool Mata Hari and dismiss these thoughts, `cause if he senses just the slightest hint of fear you might as well kiss your ass goodbye." With that in mind I jumped right back into my role with, "Mohammed words can't express how pleased my heart is over the incredible contributions you are personally making toward world peace. And the way you have been able to leap over the numerous obstacles your organized peace talks have encountered, is an astonishing tribute to your own brilliance, and the love

Forbidden Child III Exposed

you hold for all humanity. What I can't understand is why Israel outright refuses to bargain on the Jerusalem issue?"

He shook his head as he replied, "I don't understand it either. All they have to do is agree to allow Arab citizens free movement in the city of Jerusalem, and we could sign the most promising treaty for peace the world has ever known."

The moment he finished speaking, I lifted his hand to meet my lips, then tenderly kissed it just once and said, "I told you over the phone, you have found a special place in my heart Mohammed, and if there is anything I can do to help you get your peace treaty signed, please don't hesitate to ask."

He smiled softly and with a gentle voice replied, "Thank you for sharing that Christina, because knowing I'm in your heart, fills my heart with joy." He said those words with such sincerity that as we walked on I thought, "My God, could I possibly be wrong about this man?"

Just then we reached the dining room, where Mohammed turned to me with the cutest smile and said, "I hope you brought your famous appetite, because I had a feast fit for a king and queen prepared."

Our dinner arrangements were more than just fit for royalty, they were obviously ordered to be as romantic as possible, with a candle lit table, flowers, champagne, and soft music. When we reached the table Mohammed very gallantly, pulled out my chair then proceeded to pop the cork from a champagne bottle.

He poured two glasses to the rim, handed one to me, and as we toasted he said, "I raise my glass to the most incredible woman I've ever met." I smiled graciously as we sipped from each other's glass.

Then I gave him the most sincere look I could

muster and replied, "My sentiments are mutual."

He looked at me with admiration in his eyes and said, "I want you to know I've seen your latest film, and I found myself quite impressed with the message your film carried.   So I decided to have a tape of your concert performance sent to me, and I was even more impressed by the crusade you have begun to save our planet's environment."   He took my hand in his and added, "Christina, I believe if we joined forces for peace and a cleaner environment, then the two of us could actually save this planet."

My eyes lit up the room as I squeezed his hand and excitedly replied, "Oh, Mohammed. I was hoping you would feel that way, because I wanted to talk to you about doing just that."

He looked at me inquisitively and asked, "What did you have in mind?"

I stood up from my seat, then taking his hand in mine, I knelt beside him and said, "Just this Mohammed, in two weeks I will be taking my concert on an international tour, and I'm doing it because I want to bring my environmental message to the entire world. The only obstacle keeping me from accomplishing my goal is the League of Arab Nations, because all of them, including Saudi Arabia, have denied my request to perform a live concert in your nations."

"I know of the request you made," he interrupted. "The reason your requests were denied, is because it is forbidden by Muslim law to allow any type of public performance to take place in our nations at all."

This time I interrupted with a look of delight, "Mohammed, please just hear me out! Besides going on an international tour, I have also arranged for my first concert which is scheduled to take place in Israel on March 15th,to be televised live to every nation on earth.

Forbidden Child III Exposed

Except of course for the Arab Nations; they also refused to air my concert. Now what I'd like to propose is that you as the leading member of The League of Arab Nations, use your influence with your Arabian brothers, and convince them to allow me to perform in their nations." Immediately he pulled his hand out of mine, and for one split second I caught that old familiar look of pure evil anger radiating from his eyes.

Then just as fast he plastered a patronizing smile on his face, and with a chuckle said, "That's preposterous, Christina. Don't you realize what you're asking me to do is completely unheard of in the Arabian world?"

I stood to my feet and calmly replied, "Frankly, Mohammed, I'm disappointed with your condescending attitude. Don't you realize what you're asking Israel to do is completely unheard of as well?"

Looking him straight in his eyes I added, "Please tell me how you expect Israel, the Western world, and myself to truly believe the Arabian world is honestly leaving the ways of the past behind, if your nations won't even allow your citizens to view a live performance on their own television sets?"

His eyes opened wide with that little bombshell, then he began shaking his head again as he looked at me curiously and said, "You know, you may be right."

I jumped right on that one as I knelt back down and excitedly said, "Just picture it, Mohammed. You and I standing together in the Holy City of Mecca, beaming our images to the entire world as we proclaim our mutual desire for world peace and a cleaner environment." I could see the wheels turning in his head.

Then all at once he embraced me lovingly and said, "I'll do it!"

Forbidden Child III Exposed

When I left for home that evening I took with me the knowledge that on March 14, 1998, I would once again be performing a live concert on Saudi soil. Only this time, the entire Arabian world would be watching! As James drove me back to our home on the Powers Complex, I thought, "Oh well my dear Mohammed, I guess soon enough I'll know for sure if you're truly sincere, or if you're as full of shit as I think you are." Just then we pulled into the driveway and three very anxious men came running out to greet us.

The first thing I said with a presumptuous smile and a devious look in my eyes was; "Mission accomplished, guys."

CHAPTER 17

For the entire two weeks before leaving for Saudi Arabia, I tried desperately to convince Michael to stay home with Taylor.   That way he would have at least one parent with him in case our plans backfired.   But he and Frank outright refused to allow me to go on this mission alone.   And to tell you the truth, when we got off the plane at the Mecca International Airport, and I saw all the armed guards waiting to take my entourage and me to the king's palace, I was more than happy they were with me.   Mohammed was more than cordial when we arrived at the palace, especially to Michael.

He seemed to be sizing Michael up with every look as they talked, and at the same time he almost totally ignored me, which was fine until I heard him say, "Christina has informed me you will all be leaving for Israel right after her performance tonight, but I was hoping I could persuade you and your wife to stay over as my guests and leave in the morning.   This way you and I might get to know one another a little better."

I didn't even give Michael the chance to open his month before I interrupted with, "Mohammed, I've already explained to you my itinerary is planned right down to the very last minute, so why would you think my husband could change it?"

He looked at me as if I were totally out of line

then turned to Michael and said, "Does your wife always speak for you?"

Michael politely answered, "Only when she's running the show, and this happens to be her show."

Mohammed turned back to me and said, "Won't you please accept my invitation to stay the night, Christina?"

I smiled sincerely and answered, "We'd love to stay Mohammed, but to be honest with you the reason we can't was meant to be a surprise for you."

He looked at me curiously, "You're leaving immediately after your performance is a surprise for me? I don't understand."

This time I smiled mischievously, "I guess I can tell you now. I have an 8:00am meeting with Prime Minister Guron tomorrow morning, and after tonight's concert I'm sure I'll be able to convince him to sign the Peace Accord with Palestine."

His expression showed his approval as he excitedly replied, "You're truly a remarkable creature, Christina, and you never cease to amaze me."

I chuckled confidently, "You haven't seen anything yet. Now I'm going to ask you gentleman to excuse me while I make sure everything is set for tonight's performance."

When I walked out on the stage that night to perform the first live performance ever to be viewed by the Arabian nations and televised worldwide, I was not surprised at all to see an audience composed of fifty thousand male chauvinist pigs. I proceeded to give them a one hour show that went down in history. Immediately after my performance I invited Mohammed to join me on stage, where we jointly proclaimed our desire to achieve world peace and a clean environment for all.

Forbidden Child III Exposed

Once I had Mohammed and the entire audience agreeing with my every word, I knew it was time to drop my bombshell. So I enthusiastically grabbed Mohammed's hand and said, "Thank you so much my friends and I want to say a very special thank you to King Fehd for inviting me to entertain for everyone this evening. I love you all and I want to say that King Fehd and I see is a future world where women are treated as equals throughout the world."
woman. For it is time woman all over the world unite as one unbeatable force to fight against oppression, chauvinism, discrimination, and the brutality that is perpetrated against us by what has always been a male dominated world."

Immediately Mohammed pulled his hand out of mine and walked off the stage as the entire, stunned, audience began to boo and jeer! Only I wasn't finished yet.

I deliberately stood there and shouted over the screams of, "Stone her! Stone her!" With, "what type of people is it that will proclaim their desire for world peace, and yet continue to enslave their mothers, sisters, and daughters?"

That's when the cameras went off and the heavy curtain came down right on my head knocking me to the floor. When I stood up, I could hear the objects which were being thrown by the audience hitting the outer side of the curtain, and before I could even get my balance, Mohammed ran toward me grabbed my arm and began to drag me off the stage.

Once we were back stage he flung me up against the wall and shouted, "That was not a wise move you stupid bitch!" He raised his fist and just before he struck my face, Michael leaped on him with such force they both went flying into the orchestra pit. I screamed in horror as guards tackled Michael from all directions and began to beat him with Billy clubs.

Mohammed turned and started heading toward me with fury in his eyes and just as he reached me Frank came out of what seemed like nowhere and landed right on top of Mohammed.

Without a second thought I smashed a violin over one of the guard's head, grabbed his gun, fired it twice in the air, then lunged toward Mohammed and shouted, "The next shot is right between your King's eyes!"

Mohammed instantly looked me in the eyes, and knowing I meant it, he shouted, "Guards, cease immediately!" Once they stopped beating Michael and Frank, Mohammed ordered, "Now bring them up here!" Then turning back to me he calmly continued, "If you pull that trigger Christina, none of you will get out of this country alive."

Looking as ruthless as the devil himself I coolly replied, "I don't want to kill you Mohammed, but you're not going to kill my husband either. And I know you don't want the entire free world after your ass for killing me, now do you?"

He instantly turned the charm back on and said, "Please forgive me for my outburst, but you really should have discussed your views on equal rights for women with me before making such controversial public statements to the Arab world. Do you realize the amount of heat I'm going to get from Arab leaders for what you've done?"

I placed the gun down and said, "I'm sorry Mohammed, but if we're going to work together for a brighter future, then I had to know that future also includes the liberation of women as well."

When we were finally safely in the air, I looked at Michael and Frank who were obviously still very shaken up, and started to laugh so hard I nearly fell out of my seat.

They both looked at me as if I were nuts, then Michael threw his pillow at me and said, "You were nearly killed, I have two black eyes, your whole crew was scared to death, you almost had to shoot the fucking king, and you're laughing!"

I finally composed myself and smugly answered, "We may have taken some lumps tonight, but it's nothing compared to the lumps he's getting from his Arab brothers right now. As a matter of fact, I won't be surprised if Muslim women all over the world are marching for equal rights as soon as the sun comes up."

Frank started to laugh as he said, "Did you see the look on his face when you started shooting? I thought he was going to shit in his pants."

With that the three of us began laughing and when we finally stopped, I sarcastically said, "Step one in our mission to get the king is accomplished, step two is yet to come."

The next morning the free world was raving, the Arab world was ranting, and Mohammed was scrambling to hang onto his strong hold by releasing a public statement which read, **"I am in complete agreement with Christina Powers' desire to liberate the women of the world. But we in the Arab world realize that such a dramatic change cannot take place overnight."**

While he was very nicely covering his ass, I was preparing to set stage two in motion. Only stage two didn't go as well as I had hoped. When I tried to persuade Prime Minister Guron that Mohammed was not to be trusted, he looked at me in a condescending way and said, "Ms. Powers, just because King Fehd is not willing to bring the Arab world's view on women's rights into the twenty first century tomorrow; does not mean I'm going to cancel the most promising peace talks we've ever held with our Arab neighbors."

With that slap in the face I stood up and angrily said, "Why you arrogant asshole. I'm telling you he's plotting against your Nation's people, and you think I'm trying to sabotage the peace talks because he's a chauvinist pig." His mouth was just about to hit the floor so I added, "And if you're stupid enough to sign his peace accord, then you deserve everything you get." I turned walked to the door and slammed it on my way out.

From that day on I dove into the rest of my six month world tour, and while I was doing everything possible to stay in a positive public light, so was my adversary. Mohammed had worldwide attention as he played the perfect king of peace. He was so good at playing peacemaker that on September 3rd, 1998, the day we returned home and the same day Tom Davies confirmed our suspicions that the Arab nations were conspiring with the nation of China to undermine the economies of the West, the nations of Israel, Palestine, and Saudi Arabia were signing an historic Peace Accord which would take twenty years to implement completely and it also gave Mohammed everything he wanted. That night we began calculating the current rate at which Mohammed's plans were proceeding and we figured that by the year 2020, he could have his temple completed and be ready to bankrupt the West at the same time.

So the next morning I got Barbara on the line and said, "Hi, Barbara, would you please do me a little favor?"

"Sure, what is it, Christina?" She answered.

I very calmly said, "Have the League of Women's Voters help me get on the ballots across the

country for President?"
And you know what she said, **"YES!!   YES!!"**

CHAPTER 18

After my talk with Barbara the night of September 3rd, 1998, I turned to Michael, Jimmy, Pierre, and Frank, who were sitting with me, and looking at them with the most earnest expression, I said, "It really starts now guys! Because this isn't just a race for the Presidency, this is a race for all humanity!" My heart went out to them, as they gazed back at me with the expressions of four frightened little boys.

Then Jimmy, with full dramatics seemed to sum it up for all of us, when he grabbed my shoulders and nervously said, "Oh my, God! Christina, this is scary shit! Why is all this happening?"

Sadly I shook my head, "I don't know Jimmy, but I do know this game Mohammed is forcing us to play is for keeps, and we have got to win it!"

With that, Michael hugged us both, as he pulled Pierre and Frank into an embrace of five, and said, "By the grace of God and the power of God within us, we will win." Then we proceeded to humble ourselves before the throne of God, like the five little children we truly were.

When we finished praying, Michael looked at the rest of us as if he were ready to leap into the lion's den, then while pulling up his sleeves he eagerly said, "Well, what did Barbara say?"

I smiled at Michael's willingness to get started,

especially after knowing how he once felt about the subject. Then I slightly chuckled, as I answered, "She was screaming 'Yes, Yes,' in such a frenzy, I thought she was going to have a heart attack. I didn't get it all, but I'm pretty sure she said, she'll be flying in around 7:00pm tomorrow night, and don't forget to have dinner ready!"

Barbara showed up at our door for dinner as promised, and this time she brought with her three colleagues from the League of Women Voters. After Barbara introduced Mary, Vicky, and Tanya, to Michael, Taylor, and me, she said, "Christina, we've come together to formally invite you on behalf of the League of Women Voters, to announce your candidacy for President to the country, at our annual convention next month in Washington, D.C.."

Smiling I replied, "I thank you ladies very much, but before I can accept your gracious invitation, I would like all of you to know exactly where I stand on the issues first."

Barbara returned my smile with a big one of her own and replied, "Well then start talking girlfriend, 'cause we're here to listen!"

I hugged her warmly and answered, "I think it can wait until after we have dinner." With that the two of us began to laugh, as I led them to the dining room for one of Carmen's famous lasagna dinners.

Immediately after dinner, Michael and I invited the four of them into the den. For the next five hours I proceeded to fill them in, and answer their questions on exactly where my campaign would stand, on as many of the issues we could possibly cover in one evening.

Once all the main topics were discussed, Barbara began shaking her head. Then looking at me as if I were out in left field, she said, "Girlfriend, are you getting in

Forbidden Child III Exposed

the race to win it, or is this a joke?"

I looked back at her as if she were the crazy one and answered, "Of course I want to win, I'm not running for President because I have nothing better to do!"

Shaking her head again she replied, "Well then you better tame your rhetoric a little. If you give the Democratic and Republican Party's ammunition like that to use on you, then you're not going to have a chance in hell of winning this thing!"

I started to chuckle with a slightly sarcastic tone as I answered, "I don't believe this. You're the one who convinced me that dramatic changes had to be made to save our world, and now you're telling me my language is too strong!" Flinging my hands in the air I added, "Well then, what is it you want from me?"

"Christina," she calmly began. "I agree with everything you've said, and I also believe in being radical. However, if you use your campaign as a forum to try and persuade the American public we need to make all these changes within the next four years, then you will lose for sure."

With that statement I rose to my feet and said, "Barbara, I have no desire or intention of 'sugar coating' the issues for anyone. If I'm going to be President of our Nation, then everyone is going to know exactly how I plan to lead us out of this mess. Now all I want to know from the League of Women Voters, will you back me or not?"

The four of them looked at each other with bewildered expressions for a moment, then Barbara answered for them all by saying, "All the way to the White House, girlfriend."

I smiled confidently and replied, "Great! Then I graciously accept your invitation to announce my candidacy for President, at your national convention next month."

It was sometime around 2:00am, when I was finally able to get them to stop asking their questions, and because of the hour, Michael and I insisted on Barbara and the girls spending what was left of that night, in the guest rooms, instead of heading for a motel as they planned. Realizing they were being politely told it was time for bed, they reluctantly agreed to stop talking about my candidacy in order to get some sleep. But of course, the first topic over breakfast later that morning was my candidacy for President. Right after breakfast, we held another meeting to discuss my candidacy, and how 'The League' might play a role in helping me get my campaign off the ground. Only this time I had Jimmy, and my Attorney, Tom Davies join us.

We made many decisions that day on how we would proceed with getting my name on all fifty ballots, as the Independent Party's Candidate for President. But our first decision was to keep my intentions secret until after I addressed the League's Convention, on October 16th, 1998. By 6:00pm our plans were finalized and ready to be put into motion. When Barbara and the girls left for L.A. that evening, their mission was to inform every woman's group across the nation that Christina Powers would be addressing this year's convention. As for the seven of us, Michael, Jimmy, Pierre, Frank, Tom, myself, and of course Taylor, well we were going to have to 'bust some butt', if we wanted our campaign ready to go into full swing as soon as I made my speech to The League of Women Voters.

Not ten minutes after everyone left our home that evening, I received a call from my dear friend Mohammed, who called to say, "Christina, my love. Did you like the way I persuade Prime Minister Guron to sign my peace accord, even after the spectacle of your dramatic, futile attempt to convince him not to sign?"

I immediately grew angry by his superior tone, and nothing was going to make me bite my tongue this time, as I sharply answered, "If you were standing in front of me right now Mohammed, I'd slap your arrogant face!   Does that answer your question?"

Seemingly unscathed by my harshness he calmly replied, "Forgive me Christina I truly didn't call to gloat. I'm calling because I'd like to sign a peace treaty with you.   I know you were very upset after our last meeting, but that doesn't mean I'm not willing to try and help relax my Arabian Brothers' views on women's rights."

I quickly and sarcastically replied, "Oh really, Mohammed. Why haven't you stopped the way your Arab Brothers have been brutally crushing every women's movement that has risen up in your nations since my concert?   The whole world knows, the moment they attempt any type of public display of unity at all, military troops disperse them."

He answered with a slight chuckle, "These things take time Christina, I can't change the views of the entire Arab World by myself overnight.   That's why I'm calling for your help."

"My help!" I answered with a shocked tone. "What is it you would like from me this time Mohammed, to persuade these women to humbly submit to their oppressors?"

He took on that familiar tone of sincerity as he answered, "I'd like for you to come visit the women's movement your covert activity has spawned, and help me persuade them the changes they are calling for must come slowly, and without all this civil disobedience. Additionally once I have everything running smoothly between Israel and Palestine, which I hope will be sometime around September of 1999, I'd like to invite you to accompany me on a trip to Russia, Switzerland, and China. I believe if we work together on the second stage of my plan to achieve world peace; then, we could persuade the Switzerland banking establishment to help Saudi Arabia, in financing and then signing the first peace accord ever, among the Russian Republics, China, and the entire Arab World."

Just the thought of a Peace Treaty being signed between those nations brought chills to my spine, and I found myself no longer able to keep up the charade as I viciously replied, "Why you evil, beast!   You're setting the world up for the battle of Armageddon and you're actually pleased with yourself, aren't you? Well if you think I'm that stupid that I'll unwittingly help you get away with this, then you've got another thing coming!"

He started to laugh as he replied, "I figured you'd catch on sooner or later Christina, that's why I'm going to ask you one more time, right now, to leave your family and marry me.   Then you can rule the world with me as my Queen."

I nearly choked with that one as I snapped back my answer, "You really are a **sick fuck,** Mohammed. How can you honestly believe you'll get away with this?"

His laughter at my words radiated pure evil, as he ruthlessly replied, "This is my destiny Christina, and there is nothing anyone can do to stop me."

I was so angered by the expression of his wickedness that I shouted, "You Monster! Enjoy your laughter while you still can, because I promise you Mohammed, I'm going to wipe that smirk right off your face!"

He stopped laughing with that statement, and snapped back, "How dare you presume to make idle threats against me and believe you'll get away with it.

Forbidden Child III Exposed

Especially when you're nothing more than an insignificant little woman with a big mouth!   After your fiasco with Prime Minister Guron, do you still really think there's a man on this planet that would ever truly listen to what you have to say?" With that slap across the face of every woman on earth, I really lost it!

I'm sure the anger of any woman ever insulted by the condescending attitude of a male chauvinistic pig, echoed in my voice as I shouted, "I'm going to make you eat those words, you repulsive scum bag!"

His portentous interruption was sinister to say the least, as he shouted back, "If you attempt to interfere with my plans one more time Christina, I won't wait for my Temple to be completed, because I'll come kill you myself tomorrow!"

With a superior tone of my own I replied, "You just try coming near me once, you asshole and I'll broadcast the tape I just made of this conversation on every television station across the globe. Then you'll see just how quickly the plans of **mice and men** can fall apart!"

With that blow to his intelligence he angrily replied, "You release a tape of this conversation to anyone, and you can kiss your son goodbye, because I'll come after him instead of you."

I saw flames as I screamed, "Don't you dare threaten my family, because I'll castrate you myself, you bastard! And if you don't want anyone to hear what you truly have to say to the world, then I suggest you stay the **fuck** away from my family. If I so much as catch the slightest scent of your stench anywhere near us, then you can kiss your plans to rule the world goodbye, because I'll obliterate you from the face of the earth! And Mohammed, if you truly learned anything about me from watching my life unfold as you've said, then you know I don't make idle threats!"

I slammed the phone in his ear, turned to Michael who was listening the whole time, and with *fire* in my eyes said, "I'm more determined to win this race and get that sick bastard, then ever before!"

CHAPTER 19

After that call, we wasted no time getting our act together.   Before the day of the convention, we managed between the six of us, to set and keep four hundred and forty six appointments with top female and male business and government leaders throughout the country, whom I believed felt as strongly about the issues we face today, as I did. I made arrangements to go abroad for the month of August 1999, to visit the leaders of Russia, Switzerland, China, Germany, France, Italy, Turkey, England, and South Korea. Not only did I have to become President, but I had some catching up to do on the international scene as well, if I was going to beat Mohammed at playing his own game. As for Barbara and 'the girls,' well they wasted no time either, and when October 16th, 1998, rolled around, I found myself mentally preparing to read the most powerful speech I had ever written, to the largest group of women in history to ever attend a convention held by The League of Women Voters. There were eight hundred thousand women of every race, creed, and color from all across the nation, who besieged the Capital that day, and they all came just to hear what I had to say. Of course, along with the girls came the reporters, who had over the last three weeks created enough speculation over why I was appearing at the convention that year, to cause vice-president Kal to call me personally and ask, "Christina, is there any truth to the rumors you may be interested in running for a public office?"

I simply answered, "If you didn't hear it from me, Sam, then it's not true."

The next thing we knew, his wife Susan Kal had personally invited herself to address the convention, and with a little arm twisting from the White House, her address was purposely slotted to come just before mine. I was a little surprised Barbara gave in as readily as she did, but I didn't see the sense in pushing the issue if she wasn't, so we let Susan go first.

Due to the size of the expected crowds, the convention was moved from the Convention Hall, to the Washington Monument. Seated in the front row we could hear Susan quite well as she told the League's Members, at least ninety seven reasons why her husband, Vice-President Sam Kal should be our next president.

As she was finishing up her speech, I was unconsciously squeezing Michael's hand so hard, that he said, "Ouch! What are you trying to do, break my hand?"

I loosened my grip and answered, "I'm nervous, all right."

Taylor hearing this pulled my other arm down toward him until he could wrap his little arms around my neck to whisper in my ear, "Don't be nervous Mom, Dad and me are here."

A tear came to my eyes as I lovingly returned his embrace, and softly replied, "Thank you my little love. I feel better already."

Just then I looked up at the platform to see Barbara taking the podium from Susan to boisterously say, "Ladies, without any further delay, let's just welcome Christina Powers to the podium!"

I rose from my seat when their cheers filled the fresh autumn air, and as I climbed the steps to the platform I thought, "Oh well! Here goes everything, Lord!" When I reached the podium I hugged Barbara warmly, then turned to the largest audience I had ever addressed in my life and said, "I thank you for a truly heart felt welcome my sisters; and I am honored that every one of you actually dared to brave this phenomenal Washington traffic, just to hear what I have to say."

With that a loving laughter echoed throughout the park. Then raising my fist in the air I enthusiastically shouted, "Way to go, ladies!" The laughter immediately turned into cheers of self-worth, so I encouraged our moment as united women, to bask in the glory of our self-pride, by applauding the crowd and the cheers rumbled like thunder.

When we composed ourselves, I continued by saying, "And I must add, my heart is also filled with a great sense of pride in knowing that among we woman nearly two hundred thousand brothers with kindred spirits have come to celebrate a common bond, the desire to truly obtain equality for all, and in our life time!"

This time as the cheers rang out a sense of true oneness with my fellow human being exploded within my spirit, and in that instant, I knew that our souls were linked together by a divine force with an omnipotent plan for the human race. That knowledge seemed to fill me with an overwhelming sense of power, and confidence, which radiated from my very core, as I continued, "I know there are men in the world today who state that civilization and the earth we inhabit, have become so barbarically corrupted and poisoned, that our generation has lost the desire to create a better world for

Forbidden Child III Exposed

future generations, because they see no way for the human race to survive anyway. Well, what I'd like to say to those men, after standing here and feeling the power of women united in body, and spirit, to make sure there is a brighter future for our children, is get with the program guys!" And the cheers rose again!

When I was able to continue I said, "I'm going to take a moment now to share a personal story with you, I think you'll find amusing. Just recently, a world renowned male public official said to me, 'Christina, there isn't a man on earth that would ever take anything I had to say seriously, because I was nothing more than an insignificant little woman with a big mouth.' In response to that statement I'd like to say, even if it were true sir, it wouldn't matter one bit. Because whether you like it or not women voters out number male voters nearly two to one. So I invite you sir, to stick those figures, along with your crude remarks into your calculations, and see just how they compute."

And the crowd went wild! Then I added, "My dear sisters, I know that with the power of the love and compassion found in the hearts of every grandmother, mother, sister, and daughter as a gender, can accomplish what our forefathers have failed to do. That is to truly create a nation which stands under God with liberty equality and justice for all! I also believe in my heart that once we stand together to make the hard changes needed to save our world, then our grandfathers, fathers, husbands, brothers, and sons, will join our cause!"

With that they lost it again! When I finally calmed them down, I said, "Now I know there has been much said over my reasons for accepting the invitation to address this year's convention, so right now I'd like to put an end to all the speculation by saying, after many months of soul searching, my family and I have decided that I should run for office as the Independent Party's Candidate for President of the United States of America, in the year 2000!"

At that moment, the sound of the cheers of admiration and love which rang-out, had the intensity to reach every ear on earth, and put the fear of God, in the hearts of every politician in Washington, D.C.

Once I knew I had everyone's full attention, I calmed the crowd back down and continued by saying, "I believe it is way past time for our great nation to take a new direction into the future. A direction which will lead not just America, but the entire world toward a rejuvenated earth, and a renewed faith in the relentless ability of the human race to persistently rise, and meet, the challenges of the future every time. Although history has shown us the incredible capabilities of the human spirit, it has also shown us that without strong leadership set on a direct and determined course, we might not have survived to this point. Knowing this has caused me great concern, because with all the possible leaders I see on the horizon, who might one day lead our nation, I truly could not find one, I felt would be capable of leading us over the numerous obstacles, which await us all in the twenty first century. I also know first-hand, due to the corruption and deceit, many of our politicians are found involved in today, America is not what she once was. So I come before you as a fellow citizen, who knows that there is a great need to bring honesty, and a renewed conviction of integrity, back to our nation's government. This is one reason I have decided to run for President. I ask for your support of my candidacy, because I still believe **America** is the **greatest nation on earth!** With the strong leadership skills I will bring to the White House if elected, I will help to bring forth the opportunity for all of us, to make

Forbidden Child III Exposed

our powerful nation once again the most respected on earth! I also believe that together we can make the changes necessary, to bring our **Educational System** to a level which will rival the world! **Together** we can have a truly viable and fair **Welfare System**, which will enable our less fortunate citizens to live a productive and self-rewarding life! **Together** we can create a **Comprehensive National Health Care Program**, which will protect the millions of Americans who are now uninsured, and spare the fear our senior citizens feel of losing their life savings, due to an **unaffordable Health Care System. Together** we can once again have a **cleaner environment**, where we won't be drinking **polluted waters** and **breathing toxic air. Together** we can **eliminate our nation's deficit,** and if elected, I guarantee this will be accomplished within my first term! **Together** we can wipe out **poverty, hunger, malnutrition,** and the **deadly diseases** which are ravaging our world as we speak! **Together** we can overcome a history of **bigotry, prejudice, sexism, racism, discrimination,** and the disease of **ignorance,** which is prevalent within our society today! I know these things can be accomplished because **together,** we are not just mere mortals, we are **divine beings empowered by God**, which is our birth right thanks to His **unconditional gift of love.** That is why **together** we can create the miracle, which will produce a nation known for **equality, tolerance, open-mindedness,** and **fairness** for **all its citizens!** I know the challenges of the twenty first century can only be met if we have faith in one another, and believe in ourselves as a people with a **common purpose**. Once we truly decide to work together for the good of all humanity, then I know we will find the way to conquer the overwhelming burdens our nation, and the world face today. My friends, all my claims will not be merely promises blowing in the wind. This I can guarantee, if you stand with me by voting for me, and my hand picked running mates who have decided to run with me on the Independent Party's ballot, for crucial offices in the House and the Senate. By asking for your vote for myself, and my hand picked running mates, I am inviting you to join us in the **greatest**, **peaceful revolution** this nation, and world, has ever known. And I promise, if you will allow me the opportunity to lead our nation into the twenty first century, as the **first woman President of the United States of America**, then together the dreams of our people will once again have renewed life. Now I pray that the love, blessings, and power of God, be with us all as we rise **together** as **one**, to meet the **challenges** of the **twenty first century!**" Then I raised both fists in the air, and shook them triumphantly as I shouted, "**Thank you, America, God bless, and Amen!**"

With that nearly one million people leaped into the air and began cheering so loudly, that the ground rumbled! And their cheers evoked a renewed sense of hope, and optimism, for a brighter future.

All at once they began shouting a chant in unison, "Christina for President in 2000!" The sight of this breathtaking display of humanity, showing their love for me, and their faith in my ability to the entire world with enough power to reach the heavens, humbled my heart to the point of tears. Then almost as if being thrown into a bottomless pit, the realization of the awesome challenges I had just given my word I'd lead our nation through, hit me. I knew at that moment, if I had to, I would give my life to give my fellow being another chance for a new beginning.

CHAPTER 20

When we held our press conference that evening, the male reporters began firing their so called sophisticated questions at me like gang busters.

My answers remained calm, cool, and dignified until Ken Carpenter from the Washington Press, asked a question which resembled a statement of judgment, "Christina, you don't even hold an Associate's Degree from a Community College, and you expect the American public to believe you can accomplish your noble goals?"

Realizing the questions were becoming more of a challenge similar to an all-out attack of my intellect, rather than an interest in where I stood on the issues, I put my dukes up by deliberately delivering my answers so precise and fast, I had their heads spinning. "Ken, if a doctorate degree was what held the solutions to our nation's problems, then we wouldn't have all these problems to solve, now would we?" I wanted to add smart ass, but I managed to control the urge.

The next question came from Brent Bombal, "Christina, you morally proclaim your desire to bring honesty and integrity back to our government, but I have to wonder, how you can make such a virtuous claim, when the way you've obtained your empire, Powers Incorporated, looms under a shroud of deceit and possibly chargeable criminal activities?"

"Brent, your question sounds more like an accusation, that I may have committed a crime, or crimes, to have accomplished the incredible task of rising from the ashes of a crushed life, to be standing where I am this evening. And frankly sir, that angers me!   So to put an end to this kind of nonsense, right now I plainly state, I will not hide my past business tactics from anyone. And I guarantee, you will not find a skeleton in my closet America isn't already familiar with." Then I boldly stood in front of a room full of hungry reporters and said, "Gentleman, due to your rude manipulation of this interview from your female colleagues, I think it's time to say goodnight."

As I turned away Brent yelled, "Christina, you haven't answered one question on the issues, and you're dodging the press already?"

I turned back to him and calmly answered, "If you recall Brent, I wasn't asked one question on the issues. Now I'd like to thank you gentleman for the enthusiasm you've shown over my candidacy." Then I turned away and headed for the door, but they still refused to stop screaming their questions at me as I walked past them.

The press was still on my heels when I reached my entourage, who were all standing at the exit door of the conference hall, with stunned expressions on their faces. The whole frantic scene caused me to smile almost to the point of laughter as I said, "What's the matter with you guys, seen a ghost?"

With that, Barbara shook her head as if to rattle her brains loose. Then with frustration in her voice, and in front of all the reporters who were breathing down my neck she said, "What happened to your diplomacy, Christina? Did you think it would be a wise move to throw it out the window tonight?"

I simply hugged her warmly as I lovingly, yet seriously replied loud enough for all to hear, "Barbara, this isn't Hollywood, and we're not here to win a popularity contest. This is the future of the human race, and we're here to try and save it." Then I turned as I looked at everyone there and added with a sense of urgency, "This isn't a party! The survival of our future on this planet is at stake, and if I'm going to lead our nation in a last minute attempt to save it, then I cannot be intimidated by anyone or anything. I refuse to diminish the gravity of the situation one bit. Everything is going to be placed on the table, so the voters can see for themselves just what we're truly facing. If the country doesn't like what I believe we need to accomplish together in order to succeed, then the ultimate decision on the direction this nation takes, will be theirs to make. I truly believe because of this I will win, but whether I win or lose, at least I will have tried with all my heart to do something about it."

Then Sharon Peach, a reporter for the Sever Hundred Club politely asked, "Christina, one question please?"

I smiled gently as I replied, "Of course."

"You come across as a Christian woman and yet you say it's up to us to save ourselves. My question is how can you say that, when you know that Christ will return to do that himself?"

I smiled at her spiritual innocence and warmly replied, "I'm not disputing your beliefs, but I also know God is already here within us, and I believe He has been trying to do just that through us for centuries. What I'm saying, is that I'm sure when He makes his presence known, He'd rather find us working together as one to save the gifts He is giving us, then working apart to destroy them." Still looking at everyone I added, "Now that was the last question I will take tonight. Thank you." When I turned to leave that time, they were all so speechless by my statements, they couldn't have remembered their next questions if they tried.

The following morning October 17th, Taylor, Michael, the entire gang, and I, hit the campaign trail with intensity, as we began the most vigorous campaign schedule ever. The crowds we drew were so large that we stole the headlines from the major political Party's' candidates for the next two weeks, with headlines like, **"Within three days of her speech, Christina Powers has received over thirty million signatures throughout the country, and her name has now officially been placed on all fifty ballots as the Independent Party's, nominee for President."** But when the republicans stole the headlines back, they stole them back big time with headlines that read, **"Republican General Norman Howal, announced today his bid to be the first black President of the United States of America. Then he said, "I have already chosen New Jersey Governor Sheri Burns as my vice-presidential running mate, and she well be hitting the campaign trail with me as such.""** Two weeks later the Democrats struck back with headline news of their own, **"Vice-President Sam Kal announced today that he has chosen California Senator Ann Brown to be the first black female candidate to run for the office of vice-president in the history of the Democratic Party."**

When I stole the headline's back, I wished I hadn't, because they were all similar to this one, **"The Senate has subpoena Christina Powers to appear before a Senate Hearing, called to investigate possible tax evasion and questionable Wall Street**

business dealings.   The Senate has also barred Christina Powers a place on the American ballots until the investigation is completed." Beneath the headlines it read, "**We haven't even reached 1999, or the primaries yet, and the race for 2000 is gearing up to be the most dramatic in American history.**"

The morning after my forty fourth birthday, December 11th, 1998, I found myself and my attorney Tom Davies, pushing our way through a mob of reporters, as we walked down the so-called American Halls of Justice, to appear before a Senate Hearing. When we entered the Senate Chambers, the press was kept out by security, and we were promptly informed by a clerk, "The Senate Commission has decided to hold a closed hearing in order to avoid press frenzy."

My reply to her was, "On just whose authority was this decision made?"

A familiar voice from behind answered for her, "As Speaker of the House, I made that decision, Christina." I swiftly turned to see Senator Edward Kenney standing behind me, and seated behind him were eleven of the most crooked old goats in Congress.

For a moment I had to fight back my laughter at this menacing sight, then I calmly replied, "Hello, Edward." Of course I graciously nodded my head at his gang of cut throats as I added, "Good morning gentleman." I smiled sincerely and continued, "I hate to be a bother, but we already have a problem. You see a closed hearing is unacceptable to me, so right now I would like to informally and respectfully, request an open hearing?"

Their smug faces grew sterner as Edward answered for them all, "I'm afraid we've already made our decision Ms. Powers, so your request is denied."

I simply said, "You don't really think I'm going

to let you gentleman get away with this witch hunt without the public watching, now do you?" I slightly snickered as I added, "I happen to remember my rights, and if you want me to appear here, then I want you to provide me with an open forum."

Edward answered quickly, "Then I'm afraid you're going to have to make your request formally Ms. Powers, and until then I suggest we proceed with the hearing."

With that Tom interjected, "I can give you a formal request right now, sir."

Edward sternly replied, "Mr. Davies, your request will have to be made through the proper channels, and to each one of us individually."

Tom responded with wide eyes, "But that could take weeks sir and you are beginning this investigation today."

Without changing his demeanor once, Edward answered, "I'm not discussing this any further Mr. Davies, now let's begin."

I then turned and began to walk away and when I did, Edward cleared his voice and deeply said, "We have a subpoena Ms. Powers, if you try to leave I'll hold you in contempt. And I really don't think you want the voters to see me have to do that," sarcastically he emphasized, "now do you?"

I turned back and answered, "I'll answer your subpoena Senator Kenney, as soon as I return from the ladies room." I sarcastically added, "Or does your subpoena exclude that as well?"

When I entered the ladies room, I made one call to Pierre on my cell phone, and then headed straight for the hall where the press was waiting. When I opened the door, the reporters were caught off guard by seeing me emerge from the hearing so soon, but they regrouped quickly and dashed to my side. Once I had their attention, I promptly informed them just how the Senate Commission was deliberately attempting to violate my civil rights, by denying my informal request for an open hearing. Then I added, "Right now I'd like to publicly give the Senate Commission notice that at this very moment, a formal request to immediately hold open hearings is being faxed to everyone on the commission. It states, '**If my request is not swiftly granted I will institute a lawsuit against the Commission, as well as the entire United States Senate, for violating my Constitutional Rights as an American citizen.**' I've taken these strong steps because I'll be damned, before I'll allow this Commission to attempt to falsely crucify me behind closed doors. Now if you will excuse me, the hostage must return to this illusion of Congressional Justice."

When I reemerged in the Senate Chambers, I watched in total amusement and dismay, at the mentality of these self-appointed judges, as they tried to nonchalantly break from their hasty conference huddle, to somehow reply to the hand delivered faxes' they had received while I was in the ladies room. When we were all calmly settled, Edward with an amazed look on his face said, "What's the meaning of this, Ms. Powers?"

I simply answered, "Come now gentlemen, it's bad enough you don't know the Bill of Rights, don't tell me none of you can read either."

With that Tom choked so hard he almost spit his coffee all over the Senate Chambers, then I added, "Please Senators, just open the doors to the press and hopefully I won't have to make this farce any rougher on this Commission then I already plan to."

Not two minutes later the press was cordially invited in, and when everyone was settled Senator

Kenney said, "Before we begin Ms. Powers, I must insist that you refrain from calling this Commission a farce. The mere fact that Powers Inc. has numerous subdivisions which are not publicly listed as being owned by Powers Inc., suggest that you have something to hide."

I was polite and unpretentious as I replied, "I assure you Senator, the only reason that is true, is because over the years as I've accumulated my corporate holdings, I didn't feel it necessary to broadcast that information to the entire world. I promise you though, when these hearings are concluded and I'm found innocent of all charges, I will personally have my signature placed on every payroll check which is ultimately paid by Powers Inc.."

From that moment on the whole country had an unbelievable bird's-eye view, of every tax return and business transaction I ever made. After three months of their intense scrutinizing, all Edward could say for the commission when they finally finished their investigation on March 18, 1999, was, "Ms. Powers, we have undisputable documented evidence that by leaving the country for approximately two years, you evaded criminal prosecution for the tax evasion of your 1972/1973 tax returns."

With that accusation I immediately rose from my seat and swiftly replied, "Senator, this Commission knows quite well that I was never charged of a criminal act, because at the time my then Uncle, 'Frank Salerno' had total 'Power of Attorney' over all financial affairs. We both know if anyone were to have been charged for tax evasion, then Frank was the one legally liable. Since you had the audacity to cast a shadow of doubt over that incident, I remind the Commission that it was I whom two years later paid those taxes along with all the

**

fines that accompanied them, and in full!"

With indignation he replied, "We're not done yet, Ms. Powers. There is also the charge of insider trading in reference to the day you brought Wall Street to its knees, as you so ruthlessly acquired the controlling interest of three major American corporations. Until you can prove to the commission that you had no previous knowledge of that day's events, you will still be barred from your place on the American ballots."

I held myself with dignity as I replied, "With all due respect Senator, I was investigated at that time and cleared of all charges. You know as well as I do, all I did that day was capitalize on the selfish greed of big business. And please correct me if I'm wrong Senator, but wasn't one of your family's corporations one of those I acquired that day?"

At that moment with heartless frustration he tossed his gavel down and said, "Case dismissed!"

Even the press cheered for me after that. They continued cheering for me right through their nightly news broadcasts that evening, with reports similar to the one Tom Broly gave on NBC, "Christina Powers disgraced the Senate Commission today as she triumphantly wins the right to remain on the American ballot, as the Independent Party's candidate for President. When asked how she felt about the decision, she enthusiastically replied, 'Vindicated. Now hopefully the Senate will allow us to truly concentrate on what's really important, like the issues.' Then to add insult to injury, not two hours later she kept her promise to the Senate Commission, by having her signature stamped on an incredible four hundred and seventy two thousand payroll checks from all across the country. As it turns out, now that all the corporations held by Christina Powers are being listed under the one name of

Forbidden Child III Exposed

Powers Inc., Christina Powers is second to only King Mohammed Fehd of Saudi Arabia, for the title of the wealthiest entrepreneur on the face of the earth. To top it off, her holdings are the most financially successful and environmentally conscious in the world, with corporate names like Tord Automotive, Easting House Electronics, Kenney Baby foods, Bradford Computers, and the Mitsubisa Corporation of Japan, just to name a few of her credits. It's now known that it was Powers Inc. which was truly behind last year's two hundred billion dollar Mitsubisa Corporations takeover of the Model Oil Company of Dallas, Texas. Then upon close examination of the corporations actually controlled by Christina Powers, we've discovered they lead the world's industries across the board, with salaries, and benefits for their employees, and boast the highest employees' satisfaction rate in the 'country.' After revealing the extraordinary magnitude of her vast holdings to the world, at a press conference this afternoon she was asked, 'What's next, Christina?' It's said she simply smiled at the reporter and stated, 'Change the world!'"

Thanks to the Commission we had three crucial months to make up. When we hit the campaign trail the next morning on March 19th, 1999, we hit it with twice the vengeance as the first time. Thanks to the commission again, the crowds that came to hear what I had to say on the issues, were also twice as large as the first time. Of course, I hit them right between the eyes with the reality of the most urgent issues of the day, as I gave speech after speech, marveling and shocking the crowds. Because everywhere I went, I clearly outlined my extremely radical solutions, on how together we could attempt to solve our nation's problems.

As for the press, well they stuck to our twenty

Forbidden Child III Exposed

bus caravan like glue, as we bounced across the country from city to city and state to state. And thanks to the press, excerpts of every speech I gave were broadcast across the nation so much, that by the time I was ready to make my trip abroad on August 1st, I was leading all my opponents in the polls by at least a twenty five percent margin.

The first stop on my trip was Russia, to meet with the newly elected President, Nicolai Puton in Moscow. After our cordial introductions we sat down to a six hour meeting, where I politely reminded him of all I had already contributed and accomplished over the years through Powers Inc., to the democratization of the Russian Republics. I also informed him of what I would propose to accomplish in the future between our two nations as President. After that I asked for his international support of my candidacy, and he offered it enthusiastically. Once I knew within my heart, I could trust and rely on this man as a future ally, I proceeded to fill him in on the details of the conspiracy I had uncovered between the Arab World and the Chinese Government to conquer and rule my nation and his. Upon seeing the proof for himself, he agreed to bog down his upcoming peace talks with these nations until I was in office. We could then join the political, economic, and if need be, even the military forces of our nations together, in order to put a kink in Mohammed's dream of world dominance.

Next was Switzerland, where I had a little over three hundred billion dollars in foreign and American currency stashed. When I met with President Metal, and the six members of the Federal Council, I used that little bit of clout, along with my future plans for specific joint financial ventures between our two nations. I was seeking their nation's internationally known historic support of any Republican Party's' candidate for President of the United States. After which I received their overwhelming support for my candidacy. Once again when I knew I could trust them, I showed them the same documented evidence of Mohammed's scheme, as I showed President Nicolai Puton. After they saw for themselves that Mohammed was planning to undermine their banking industry, they overwhelmingly agreed to help delay the peace talks as well.

From there it was off to meet with the leaders of Germany, France, Italy, Turkey, England, South Korea, Japan, and of course China. I wanted to explain to each of them individually, what I would propose to accomplish economically, and environmentally, between their Nations and America, if I were President. I also wanted to feel out the Chinese leaders, and I didn't like what I felt.

Three weeks into my trip, I was informed that my friend King Mohammed had just made a surprise visit to the States; where on the White House lawn he loudly proclaimed, "I have come on behalf of the Leaders of the Arab world, and the Nation of Israel, to show our support of Vice-President Sam Kals, candidacy for President. We throw our full support behind his campaign, because he has proven to us and the world, that he is a man of his word, when he helped mediate the now historic Peace Accord between Israel and Palestine." I was also informed that after his speech my lead in the polls dropped substantially, but when I returned home on September 3rd with the international support of the leaders of every nation I met with, except China, the polls bounced back quite nicely.

CHAPTER 21

After our trip, we took two days to recuperate at the Powers Headquarters. The day I was getting ready to go back on the campaign trail Frank and Tom entered my office, and with a look of confusion Tom said, "Christina, we have a problem, the New York State Election Committee has rejected your birth certificate. The Commissioner called me personally and said he was so confused that his staff could not find your records that he decided to research your birth records himself. It appears your birth certificate which was filed with the county clerk's office never had the hospital stamp on it and when checked with the birth hospital there is no record of your birth. On further investigation your birth record was never listed with the State of New York. Since he could not validate your birth certificate, he said he has taken your name off the ballot until this issue is resolved. Do you have any idea why they can't find your birth records?"

I was stunned and it showed on my face as I gasped, "Oh my God." I stood up from my desk so quickly that I had to grab the edge to steady myself because I became lightheaded.

Frank grabbed my arm, "Christina are you alright?"

When the color finally came back to my face I looked at him with a bewildered expression and said,

Forbidden Child III Exposed

"No Frank I'm not and you're right we do have a problem, a big one that I'm not sure how to handle. Talk about being blind-sided, I never saw this one coming."

Tom shook his head, "I don't get it Christina, what kind of problem could there be with your birth records?"

Just then Michael burst into the office, "Christina I was just asked by a reporter why your birth records cannot be found."

"I know honey; Tom and Frank just informed me."

Michael gave me a confused look as he asked, "What happened? I thought your birth certificate was legal."

"I thought so too, but I guess mobsters don't know how to legalize a fraudulent birth certificate."

Frank, shaking his head said, "What are you guys talking about? Why would you have a fraudulent birth certificate?"

I looked at Tom and Frank who both had dumfounded looks on their faces and I started to laugh just a little as if I had just gone a little crazy and said, "You guys had better sit down for this one. It's like this, I was never born Christina Valona. A few years ago I discovered that shortly after my birth my mother had Frank Salerno 'doctor' my birth certificate to conceal my true parent's identity in an attempt to keep me safe. With everything going on it never even crossed my mind that the counterfeit birth certificate was not legally registered with the state or I would have never submitted it."

Tom cleared his throat, "Christina two questions, do you have your authentic birth record and were you born in the States?"

"Yes Tom I do and I was."

"Well then as your attorney it's a very simple fix, I'll just submit your original birth certificate and we go on. In this case, it doesn't matter who your parents are as long as your records are legal, besides the world knows you as Christina Powers anyway."

Frank interjected, "Tom did you hear her, she said her mother had Frank Salerno 'doctor' her birth certificate to conceal her true parent's identity in an attempt to keep her safe." Then, he gave me a very concerned look as he continued, "Christina why would the identity of your true parents put you in danger?"

I sighed with a sense of utter defeat and said, "At this point guys if I have to reveal who my true parents are I don't think this campaign is going to ever get on the road. Tom is there any way you can get the counterfeit birth certificate legally registered?"

He shook his head and chucked, "Christina you're trying to become the first woman President of the United States of America; do you really think we could get away with that?"

"No Tom I don't, I just didn't want to reveal my true identity, but I guess in order to do what I know I have to do to keep my family safe then once again I have no choice. I have to reveal to the world whose 'forbidden child' I am. I only discovered the truth after Frank's murder trial. I learned then that my mother was Norma Jean Montensel and my father was John Fitzgerald Kenney and I was named Christina Kenney."

A look of shock came over them both then Frank said, "Are you telling us that you are Marilyn Monrow and JFK's daughter?"

Just then Pierre buzzed me on the intercom, "Excuse me Christina, but we seem to have a problem, may I come in to speak with you?"

"Sure." I answered with a disgusted tone already anticipating the problem.

Pierre wore a look of total confusion when he entered my office, "Christina we've been getting hundreds of calls from reporters all over the world asking why you submitted a fraudulent birth certificate to election bureaus all over the country. I don't know what to tell them. Do you have any idea what they're talking about?"

I shook my head with utter frustration as I said, "I don't have any choice, I have to go public now. Pierre please call a press conference for 6:00pm this evening in our main conference hall."

Michael interrupted, "Christina are you sure this is the safest thing to do? You could end up having fanatics coming out of the woodwork after you."

"Michael it's too late already, I have to go public. If I don't I'll have to drop out of the race. I'll look like I'm guilty of something for hiding my true identity and now that the reporters know it won't be long before one of them finds out on their own. Either way, the political parties are going to crucify me. As for the fanatics coming after me, I'm sure Frank and his security team can handle keeping me safe." I turned back to Pierre, gave him a confident wink, "Go ahead Pierre call the press conference, I'll be ready with something to say by then."

As Pierre left the room Frank said, "Christina, I still don't get it, how can you be Marilyn Monrow and JFK's daughter when Marilyn never had a child."

"My mother never had any children she wanted the world to know about Frank. She had very good reasons for concealing my identity."

That's when Tom interjected, "Do you have any idea how you're going to tell the world who you really are and still be considered a viable candidate?"

I shook my head, "Right now I don't have a clue Tom." I looked toward Michael as I continued, "Baby please tell Jimmy that I'm not going to be able to have lunch with him and Taylor today. I am going to go meditate for a while and hopefully I'll know what to say by the time I give the press conference."

CHAPTER 22

As soon as I entered the conference room the reporters started shouting questions at me like the one Tom Brokoff asked, "Christina are you going to tell us why you submitted a fraudulent birth certificate to the election committees all over the country?"

I climbed the podium and immediately had to regain control of the all the reporters shooting questions at me, and the first thing I said was, "This is a press conference people.   Now please take the seats provided each of you and we'll get this press conference started."

The place began to quiet down so I said, "Ladies and gentleman I have called this press conference to explain to the American Public the incident concerning my missing birth record and why my birth certificate cannot be found.   First, as everyone knows I was raised Christina Valona by Frank Salerno a man I believed at that time was my biological uncle.   Shortly after his death, I discovered that this was not true.   I learned from my dear friend Barbara Goldstein that my mother had Frank Salerno 'doctor' my birth certificate to conceal my true parent's identity in an attempt to keep me safe. That night I discovered Barbara had been a close friend of my mother's and she felt that after Frank's death it would be safe for me to learn who my true parents were. She gave me an envelope and inside was the original copy of my birth certificate with some pictures of my mother and me along with a letter from my mother to me explaining why she did what she did.   I am at this very moment having copies of my true birth certificate hand submitted to election committees all across this country and shortly to all of you right here in this room.   I feel the only way I can truly explain to my fellow American's why I continued to hide my true identity is to read the letter my biological mother, 'Marilyn Monrow' wrote to me two weeks before her untimely death."

The gasps of shock and disbelief echoed throughout the auditorium.   Knowing that the entire country was doing the same thing, I swallowed my fear hard as I said, "Please, please allow me to continue and then I will answer your questions."   When the room quieted down I began to read,

"My beautiful Christina, I instructed Barbara, my longtime friend, to give you this letter in the event of my death. You see my darling daughter, I am your real mother and have spent all these many years watching you grow up, but afraid to approach you for fear that your father and his family would endanger your safety in some way. I met your Dad at a dinner party and we were immediately attracted to one another. In time we began a secret affair because your father was already married. He led me to believe he would leave the marriage for me. Only we discovered that his family and his father's political ambitions for your dad would not permit that to happen.   I had just discovered that I was carrying you, when your father stated that we could never be together and our affair would have to remain a secret, he said, "The world can never know." At that moment, I became afraid to tell him about you. You see your father was a United States Senator and came from a very rich and powerful family. I knew they were capable of taking any action to protect their son's

Forbidden Child III Exposed

political aspirations and I had to keep you safe.

I know the world will say that I was just another dumb blonde sex-symbol, but I am far from that my sweet Christina. I didn't tell anyone that you were born because I was afraid for your safety. That is why I asked Frank Salerno to raise you. I turned to Frank who was my friend because he was rich and powerful. I entrusted him with you swearing him to secrecy. I knew that he could protect you and also give you a beautiful home with anything that you wanted until I could come and take you away with me. Then, your dad ran for the office of President of the United States and won. All those years I never stopped loving him and when he became President, I knew I could never tell him about you or how much I still loved him. Even though I married several times, no one replaced him in my heart. When I finally reestablished a relationship with your dad, I thought he was going to walk away from everything for me; only I discovered that was not true. It was then that the FBI began to watch my every move and I became even more paranoid about your safety. When I turned to Frank he betrayed me and I learned that he was more interested in having me as his trophy wife then being your surrogate father. When he proposed to me I was horrified and refused him. He became very angry and tried to hurt me. I ran from his house and was more determined than ever to make enough money with my next movie, so you and I could just disappear. Once again, I learned the hard way that the only person I could depend on was myself. All those people in my life who I thought really loved me, did not. They would leave me like my dad or were unable to love me like my mother who was sick and all the rest just used me.

I want you to know a little about me. All I ever really longed for was to be loved and wanted. I never

Forbidden Child III Exposed

knew my dad, and my mom was too sick to take care of me. I went from foster home to foster home until one day my mom came back for me. We were happy in our own little house, only not for long, because mom was once again hospitalized. I ended up in an orphanage until a couple came and brought me to live with them. They were very strict and mean to me. Many nights I cried myself to sleep, because I just wanted my mom back.

If you are reading this letter my sweet darling, then you know that something terrible has happened to me. I may not be able to tell you what, but I can tell you why. I am a threat not only to the Kenney family whose son is your father and the United States President, but now to Frank as well, who continues to harbor a great deal of resentment toward me, for refusing his marriage proposal.

Please know my beautiful baby girl, that you have always been the most important thing in my life. I love you with all my heart and soul. I know in my heart, that if you had the opportunity to know me, you would love me just as much as I love you. Not a moment has gone by without my wondering what you are thinking and doing. I have lots of photos of you growing up and I keep them in a secret place. Every night I take them all out and study each one carefully. I know every hair on your head, your laughing eyes, your little adorable nose and those beautiful little pink lips. How I long to hold you, how I long to kiss you, how I long to show you how much I love you. No matter what happens to me, please know that I never stopped loving you and will always be with you. I pray for you to have a far better life than I had; wherein, people will love, adore and shower you with tons of attention. One more thing my sweet angel, I beseech you not to ever reveal to the world whose daughter you really are. I fear they will come after you as well. Good bye my sweet darling,

All my love, your Mommy, Marilyn Monrow"

When I finished you could hear a pin drop. Everyone was stunned for what seemed like minutes until finally Ken Carpenter from the New York Times asked, "Christina everyone knows Marilyn Monrow never had any children and you're expecting the American public to believe you're her daughter?"

"I was asked that same question just this morning Ken and I will give you the same answer; my mother never had any children she wanted the world to know about. The reason she wanted to keep my identity secret was because she feared if anyone knew who my true parents were my life would be endangered. My mother did what she did because she loved me with all her heart."

Sam Donaldson from NBC news asked, "Christina, you submitted a false birth certificate and lied to the American people and 'the World' about your true identity; why should we believe you now?"

"That is a very fair question Sam and if you will open the envelope my staff is handing out, you will find copies of my birth certificate along with the letter I just read and photos of myself and my mother Marilyn Monrow left for me. I can assure the American people and 'the World' that my true birth record will be found and once again I did what I did because I was honoring my mother's wishes. The only reason I have come public now is because I have to in order to run for the Presidency."

Mark Hampton from CNN asked, "Christina do you still plan on running for President and if so can you tell us why should the American people believe anything you may say after this deliberate attempt to deceive the Public?"

I felt a little indignation with that one so I came out fighting as I said, "Mark I believe the American people will understand and forgive me for doing what I did. And yes I do still plan on running for the office of President. As for the American people believing anything I may say after this; well I think my record speaks for itself. I would have never dishonored my mother's wishes if I did not feel the issues our nation faces are much larger than continuing to honor my mother's wishes."

Cindi Albright from ABC news asked, "Christina it plainly states on your birth certificate that your father was John F. Kenney. Are you trying to carry on your 'father's legacy'?"

I smiled big for that one as I answered, "Cindi I can assure you my running for President to carry on my 'father's legacy' was the furthest thing from my mind when I made my decision to run. I am running for the office of President of the United States of America for one reason; and that is I want to help save this nation for our children's future. I believe if drastic steps are not taken soon to make our America great again, then we will no longer be the beacon of hope citizens all over the world have known us to be. "

Cindi quickly came out with a follow up, "Christina one more please. I believe the American public will understand why you kept your identity secret and forgive you, but you still attempted to deceive the public for our Country's highest office. This makes me wonder what else you may be hiding from the public and I have to ask why should the American People believe you now?"

Forbidden Child III Exposed

"Fair question Cindi and I will answer as bluntly as possible. First, I give the American People my word that I am not hiding anything else about myself. Second, I attempted to continue to hide my true identity because my father was assassinated, my mother's death was suspicious, my uncle, when he tried to run for office was also assassinated, and my mother was correct that if my identity was known by certain individuals my life would be in danger. Knowing the risk I am taking with my life by revealing my true identity to the world, I still feel strongly the threats that face our nation today required me to take that risk.   I love this country and if I saw anyone I felt had the ability to lead our nation into a 21st century; then, I would not be running. As for anyone believing me, I am the CEO of successful businesses all over the world. I have stepped up to help bring the nation of Ghana from civil war and poverty to peace and prosperity. I have placed my life in harm's way to help free the international hostages in Iraq and have brought international press on nations that continue to treat woman like second class citizens. I have put the spotlight on travesties and injustices every place I saw it. I did all this because I truly care about the welfare of people all over the world. That is who I am. I give my word to the American People that I will give my all to our nation because I see what our nation and the world will face tomorrow. I want to help to make a brighter future not just for our nation's children, but for children all over the world. I know that America can overcome the numerous obstacles we face now and in the future if we have strong leadership. If we work together we will accomplish the task of maintaining our status in the world and continue to give our children the opportunities we now have as America citizens. Now, I think I've said all that needs to be said on this subject and I thank

Forbidden Child III Exposed

you all and the American People for your time."

Ken Carpenter shouted, "Christina please one more question. How do you plan on carrying out all your noble goals?"

"I will be informing the country on how I plan to do just that as soon as I get back on the campaign trail. Now that will be the last question and once again I thank you all for coming."

Then, I walked out of the room as they all scrambled to be the first to get their reports out to press.

CHAPTER 23

That night the whole world knew my true identity and let me tell you everyone had something to say about it. Even my advisory King Fehd called me on my private line and the first thing he said was, "You are the daughter of a king and you lied to me. I know who you are and I now know you know who you are and that is why I will give you one more chance to be my bride and bear my son. If you refuse me now then I will have no choice but to destroy you and everything you represent."

"What kind of moron are you? I've already told you I'm not the woman you think I am and if you threaten me one more time, I'm going to be forced to destroy you and everything you represent asshole! Now, don't call me again unless you come to your senses and are willing to work with me to make this world a better place."

"Christina I promise you will come to me on my terms or you will die."

Trying to keep my calm I simply replied, "King Fehd I promise **you** that if I see you again that will be your last day on earth. Now, I think we have said enough so good-bye."

As I went to hang up he screamed, "I will behead you for that you bitch!"

I was steaming when I got off that phone and all I

could think about was how to get this crazy bastard before he gets me; because I knew in my heart that he meant what he said.

The controversy over my true identity took the headlines for the next two weeks and when the dust finally settled I had the support of the entire country. It took another two weeks before I was placed back on the ballots in all fifty states.

Then, it was back on the campaign trail. Our first stop was, Prince William Sound, Alaska, where a crowd of over fifty thousand strong braved the chilly weather to hear me address the 'country's' environmental and energy issues. That's when I hit Mohammed, his Arabian Brothers, and the entire oil industry right where it hurts, as I revealed my alternative energy plans for Americas future by saying, "My fellow citizens, my campaign stop here, at the tragic sight of America's worst oil spill in history, **the 1989 Exxon Valdez disaster,** where ten million plus gallons of oil poured into these once pristine waters, is a symbolic stop. Because if I'm elected President, we will work to see that this type of disaster never occurs again. We would accomplish that by revamping, and then instituting an entirely new energy policy for our nation."

I received an enthusiastic round of applause, after which I continued with, "First, we would mandate that every automobile sold in the United States be electrically powered by the year 2006. This move alone would reduce 60% of our nation's phenomenal oil consumption. I know this can be accomplished, because the scientific crew at Tord Automotive has developed a prototype engine, which takes twelve hours to charge on a normal household current, and it doesn't need to be recharged until after fifty six hours of continuous use. The engine is capable of reaching top speeds of seventy five miles' p/h, is as quiet as a kitten purring, is powerful enough to pull two busloads filled with passengers up a two mile incline without losing power once, and to top it off, it's rechargeable enough while in motion to give you that fifty six hours of continual use. Although this engine sounds wonderful there are some draw backs. The first drawback is the overall cost, because to mass-produce these vehicles it will take vast capital investments. The second drawback is the price such a vehicle would cost the consumer, because a basic auto with this technology would run about forty nine thousand dollars. The third drawback is the havoc this technology will place on the American oil industry. Now, these are the three big problems we will face by doing this, but I believe it's possible to overcome these problems by doing three things. We would create an environmental/energy super fund, in which capital would be raised to fund the following: First, to give thirty year interest free loans to the automotive industry to enable them to take on such a vast overhauling of their companies without cutting into their current profit margins. Second, the fund would also be used to pay half the cost of these vehicles for the public and private industry, for the first ten years. Third, we would give thirty year interest free loans to the American oil industry, so they could revamp their companies to build and maintain America's new power supply, which will be totally provided by solar and wind power, thus eliminating another 30% of our oil consumption. This would be accomplished by allowing each company the right to line an equal share of the American interstate highway system with high power solar panels and state-of-the-art super wind powered turbine generators. These generators are sensitive enough to produce large amounts of power even when there is no natural wind flow, because they are capable of producing power from air currents created by the flow of traffic. And I would hope the American public would prefer to see this type of technology lining our highways, than the poisonous smog we will be forced to see and breathe if we don't do it. Then, the oil companies who agree to provide this new power source would be given the exclusive rights to sell this clean, efficient, energy to our nation's power plants.

To take on the extraordinary challenge of overhauling our nations' entire energy industry, from a polluting, ozone destroying, acid rain producing, petroleum dependent one, to an independent, clean, efficient one, will cost five hundred billion dollars a year for the next ten years, but it can be done. We can raise the funds to do this without overburdening ourselves, simply by putting a one dollar surcharge on every new and used auto and auto related items sold in America, for every automobile registration renewal, for every annual inspection sticker, as well as on every electrical appliance sold in this nation. By paying an extra one dollar for each of these items I have outlined, we would raise a phenomenal nine hundred billion dollars a year, and by the year 2010, we would be a totally self-sufficient, **non-polluting, energy powered nation**. There would still be an annual reserve of four hundred billion dollars, and then out of that fifty billion will go into our Nation's current national disaster fund, the environmental cleanup super fund, and the remaining three hundred billion will be placed in a holding fund to be used to improve the nation's infrastructure. Just some of the benefits we will reap from this technology will be a cleaner world to live in, and fresher air to breathe. And because we have more than enough of our own oil, to supply the rest of our oil needs, we will have a drop in our nation's trade deficit by nearly six billion dollars a year as well, due to the ceasing of all oil imports.

We would see an increase in our gross domestic product, as we sell our services and new technology abroad, because everyone in the world will want to own the electric vehicles, which only the American automobile industry will be able to provide. Thus creating a need for a threefold increase in auto workers in our nation, and they will be earning annual salaries of fifty thousand and up. And for us all as individual citizens, we will save enough a year on the price of our mass transportation, and automotive fuel bills, to more than offset the one dollar surcharges. I know what I'm proposing will be an incredible undertaking, but I also know the American People can do it. If you have the courage to join me in this venture, then I promise you, one day we will eliminate any possibility of ever having another disaster like the Exxon Valdez again." This time they cheered their approval.

At the press conference which followed my speech, I released detailed copies of my environmental/energy program, and for the next three weeks it was all anyone heard about. Before the experts could even begin to study and debate its feasibility, my opponents were calling my plan ludicrous. However, when the smoke of the controversy finally cleared, all my opponents were forced by solid documented evidence, to eat their words, and publicly admit that the plan could work.

When they did that, my lead in the polls over my closest opponents rose from a twenty five to a thirty five percent margin, and that's when my adversary King Mohammed Fehd, struck back with a statement released to the American press which read, "**After close** examination of Christina Powers' proposed environmental/energy program, I must admit with the rest of the world that it is absolutely brilliant. Although, at the same time we cannot neglect the fact that it is naively flawed. The reason I make this strong statement is it is foolish to think anyone could throw American industry into such a complete upheaval in only a ten year span, without causing major damage to the American economy as well as the economies of the rest of the world. I also believe to even suggest taking on a challenge of this magnitude in less than thirty years, shows a lack of realistic leadership skills. To help prevent this possible worldwide economic disaster, I will personally offer thirty year low interest loans to any automobile manufacturer in the world, who would be willing to mass-produce a new generation of super-efficient automobiles. If the world's auto industry would take up this offer, then we could feasibly reduce fifty percent of the world's oil consumption, as well as the pollution it causes, in a realistic fifteen years, and without leading the world into an economic nightmare. I also feel when the time does come for the world to limit its dependency on oil as drastically as Ms. Powers Gillespie has proposed, then I would hope we would turn to Geothermal Energy Plants instead of defacing our landscape."

When asked by the press to respond to King Mohammed's statements I replied, "His accusations are exactly what any oil rich sheik would want us to believe, but they are unfounded because the creation of the super fund is what will prevent an economic disaster from happening, and he knows it. Not only that, but his suggestion to build Geothermal Energy Plants all over

Forbidden Child III Exposed

the world is what truly shows a lack of realistic leadership skill. If we start drilling thousands of holes into the core heat source of the earth, it will cost the world's economy quadrillions, and it has the potential to be catastrophic for life on this planet." Even with my rebuttal, I took a seventeen percent nose dive in the polls, and when I discovered this I thought, "Touché Mohammed, but you haven't seen anything yet, because I still have a few tricks up my sleeve that will blow you away."

CHAPTER 24

The following day, October 17th, I pulled out one of those tricks by revealing my plans for America's future education/early childcare program, at a rally of one hundred thousand, where I addressed the 1999 convention of the United League of Teachers at the Meadowlands Arena in New Jersey.

I began my speech by saying, "I am honored to have been invited here today to address this convention, because from the depths of my heart, I believe that the teachers of America have chosen the most important and vital profession in our nation. At the same time my heart is saddened, because your calling has been taken for granted, abused, and neglected for nearly four decades now by our nation's leaders. I'm here to say, I think it's time it stops."

With that statement the crowd cheered and when they decided to stop cheering I said, "It boggles my mind to think that our elected leaders are allowing us to head into the twenty first century with an educational system which is in total disarray. What's worse is no one seems to know what to do about it. Well I happen to have come up with a little idea, which I believe will do more than solve the problem, because it is ludicrous to continue struggling with a flawed system when we don't have to. Right now our nation spends a mere seven hundred million dollars a year to teach fifty million

James Aiello

Forbidden Child III Exposed

American students, with only three million teachers. Then our Government has the gall to expect our three million teachers to perform miracles on the academic level.   Well I don't know about you, but I don't have to be a mathematician to know that the ratio in this equation is atrocious.   That ratio is why I've come up with a three stage proposal which will solve the problem indefinitely. The first thing we must do in stage one, is to obliterate our current education system and replace it with one that works.   Step two of stage one; we would eliminate all local school property taxes, thus returning two hundred million dollars back into the pockets of our citizens; eliminate all state contributions to their school system, thus returning two hundred million dollars back into the states treasuries.   Next eliminate all current federal contributions to the Nation's schools and channel that three hundred million dollars into our military, to give a twenty five percent across the board salary increase to everyone in our armed services.   Step three of stage one; we would create an education/early childcare superfund.   And we could create it without crushing the public financially, by simply adding a one dollar surcharge on every movie ticket, book, record, and video sold or rented in our nation.   Get ready for this folks: with this surcharge we would raise a phenomenal seven hundred billion dollars a year.   This is nearly six times greater than our current education expenditures.   Now for stage two.   First, we would triple the classroom space of our schools.   Second, we would add an additional three million teaching positions, which will fill half the additional new space we will have, and cut our student classroom sizes in half.   Third, we will increase their average annual salary from forty two thousand to sixty thousand.   Fourth, we would supply each classroom with the most sophisticated learning

Forbidden Child III Exposed

tools available today, and increase the school day by one hour. Now for stage three. First, we add another three and a half million positions into the system with starting salaries of forty thousand and up. One million more teaching positions, five hundred thousand registered nurses, five hundred thousand licensed practical nurses, another one million will be trained teachers aides and day care aides, and five hundred thousand in support staff. Second, we will place this additional staff into the remaining new space to provide early child care and preschool training to every child in America, from three months to kindergarten. We would then operate this part of our school system on a twenty four hour, seven day a week basis, and we would be capable of providing three nourishing meals a day to our children. Not only that, but there would be no charge for the day care provided, thus relieving our families of at least a four hundred dollar a month childcare expenditure. For those who choose to continue with their current child care providers, we will pay their monthly child care expenses for them, up to four hundred dollars per-month. Third, we would pay the tuition for every American who chooses to continue their education, and we will double the tuition paid to our colleges, so they could afford to provide the highest in educational standards, and increase their staff as well as their payrolls. My friends, even with all these expenditures we would still have an annual surplus in the superfund of two hundred billion dollars a year, and one hundred billion of that would go into our holding fund to be used on other programs, which I will address at a later date.

Now, to name just some of the benefits we would reap from this program. First, we would have the best school system and the most educated society in the world. Second, we would have a drop in our now 14%

unemployment rate to a 6% unemployment rate.   Third, we would have an increase in per-capita personal income, an increase in public spending, and a decrease in our public debt.   And I'm sure when you examine my entire program; you will agree that the benefits will more than compensate for the one dollar surcharge.   Now I'd like to thank you for listening and say, 'May God Bless us all!'"   And with that the crowd roared their approval.

The next day the headlines read, **"Christina Powers astonishes the nation once again, with her proposed education/early childcare program."** When the experts completed studying my proposal they all agreed unanimously, it was the most brilliant, and comprehensive, educational agenda they had ever seen. With that acknowledgment made public, my 18% lead in the polls soared to a 42% lead.   When that happened, my opponents scrambled to fight back with statements similar to the one Vice-President Kal made, "Yes it's true that *Christina Powers'* radical educational program is unique, but it is not feasible for the United States, because it is more of a socialistic approach to the problem, than a democratic one."

When asked to respond to the accusations of my critics, I answered, "My opponents may place any label they would like on my education proposal, but it won't change the fact that I'm simply using good business sense, and until I see someone come up with a better suggestion, then I'll stick with my own.   If they think my education program is radical, wait until they hear me address next months' Governor's Social Welfare Conference in Washington, D.C."

The next morning while Michael, Tom and I were working on my Citizens Care Program speech for the Governor's Social Welfare Conference it hit me like a lightning bolt and I shouted, "Oh my God I am a fucking genius!"

Michael started to laugh as he shook his head and said, "What brilliant scam have you come up with this time and how much more work is it going to cause us?"

I smiled mischievously as I said, "It's not going to cause us any extra work right now."   Then I buzzed Pierre on the intercom and continued, "Pierre please call the dynamic trio for me and have them come to my office as soon as possible."

Pierre started to laugh then said, "I assume you want Lucille, Barbara and Gloria."

I started to laugh as I said, "Is there any other?"

"You got it boss I'll send them right in."

As soon as Lucille, Barbara and Gloria entered my office I said, "Thanks for coming so quickly ladies. I have called you three in because I have a task I know only you three could pull off for me.   I want you to set up a 2000 New Year's Eve Celebration this year at the Disneyland Theme Park in Orlando, Florida.   Then, extend an invitation to all of America to celebrate the turn of the millennium with me, my family and all of our biggest name performers.   I also want to create the exact replica of the outfit my mother wore when she performed 'Diamonds Are A Girl's Best Friend'.   I want to do a tribute to her that night.   Ladies I want this to be the biggest party anyone has ever thrown and I want it broadcasted all over this country.   Are you ladies up to the task?"

They looked at each other with wide eyes at first then Lucille smiled and said, "Party, that's my middle name. You want a party; we'll give you a party."

I smiled as I said, "I knew I picked the right party girls."

As they left the room Michael said, "You don't miss a beat, do you?"

I kissed his cheek as I said, "Not if I can help it. Now let's get back to work on the Citizens Care Program."

CHAPTER 25

When the States Governor's Social Welfare Conference rolled around on November 29th, I found myself placed first on the list to address the conference, from the three top Presidential Candidates who were invited.

After a hardy round of applause, I began by saying, "I am honored to have been invited here today, and I feel privileged to have the opportunity to address such a distinguished group of Civil Servants on an issue as important as our Nation's Social Welfare Program. As we all know, it is a disaster, because we're doing nothing more than spending billions of dollars a year to keep our less fortunate citizens trapped in poverty, as we crush their spirits and devour their dignity. To the shame of us all, not only do we allow our Government Leaders to destroy the hopes and dreams of those of us who are dependent on our so-called Social Welfare Program, but we allow the Government to foster concern to 82% of our citizens who depend on Social Security benefits. Well, I for one can no longer idly stand by and watch this travesty take place without trying to stop the hypocrisy of it all. It disgusts me to think that our nation spends three billion dollars a year on the current Social Welfare Program, which breaks down to ninety million on cash benefits, seventy million on food stamp benefits, and one billion forty million on Medicaid benefits. While at the same time our Social Security Administration spends an additional seven hundred billion dollars a year in benefits, which breaks down to two hundred and fifty billion on retirement benefits, twenty billion on survivor benefits, one hundred and thirty billion on disability benefits, and three hundred billion on Medicare benefits. Then there is another twenty five billion spent on unemployment benefits, and on top of these figures we have to add six billion contributed from our employees and employers for their disability and unemployment insurance deductions. The grand total spent on all three programs from the federal, state, and the private sector is seven hundred and thirty billion dollars a year. This is why I propose to the nation a three stage plan, where the first stage would call for the elimination of all three programs as they exist today, and place them under a one blanket protection plan which we would entitle, 'The Citizens Care Program.'

In stage two we would first take five hundred billion from these funds and return it to our workers by eliminating the social security taxes. Second, we would return another six billion to the employees and employers, by eliminating their disability and unemployment insurance deductions. Third, we would return fifteen billion to our states, and relinquish them from the responsibility and expense of managing their Social Welfare Programs. Fourth, we would return the remaining three hundred and twenty billion to the federal Government to be set aside for future use. Now for stage three. First, we would create a Citizens Care super fund. Second, we would give an across the board flat rate payment of twenty thousand dollars a year to the twenty nine million Americans who are retired or disabled, which will total fifty eight hundred billion dollars a year. Third, we would eliminate all welfare benefits, because with free child care being provided, we could put the sixteen million now receiving benefits, into either on the job training programs, such as what our school systems and community action programs will offer, at starting salaries of no less then fourteen thousand dollars a year. If they choose to continue in our free education system we will give them a grant of fourteen thousand dollars a year. And as long as they maintain a B-average, we will continue the payments until they have completed their studies and enter the work force. This will add another two hundred and twenty four billion to the budget. Fourth, we would eliminate the rest of the unemployment benefits by offering the twenty two million Americans, who would still be unemployed, the same opportunity as those who were on our welfare system, at a cost of three hundred and eight billion dollars. Fifth, we would eliminate the food stamp program, because there would no longer be a need for it. Sixth, we would eliminate the medical programs, because everyone will come under our new National Health Care Program, which I will reveal at a later date. My proposal will come to a grand total of nine hundred and sixty seven billion dollars. The revenue for our new Citizens Care superfund will come from placing a one cent surcharge on every one of the two hundred quadrillion BTUs' of electrical energy consumed in our nation each year. This will raise a phenomenal two hundred trillion dollars a year. One hundred and fifty billion will come from the Federal Government's power usages, thus drawing from that reserve I mentioned, two billion from the states, five hundred billion from business, and one trillion ninety eight billion will come from household use. This breaks down to around a fifty dollar a month increase in a family of fours' average electrical bill. What we will gain from this program would be the eradication of poverty, hunger, unemployment, and illiteracy in our nation and in our lifetime. And we would still have an annual surplus in the fund of one trillion thirty three billion dollars and one trillion of that will be placed in our holding fund for uses in other programs, and it will still leave us a thirty three billion dollar surplus in the Citizens Care super fund. And I'm sure that the elimination of school taxes, and the cost of health care {which as I've said I will reveal at a later date} from the backs of our nation's businesses, will more than offset their contribution to this program. I'm also sure that the elimination in the Social Security Tax, along with the Unemployment and Disability deductions, will do the same for our working citizens.

Now I'd like to thank you for lending me your ear as I ask for your support of my candidacy, and I pray that God May Bless all our futures."

With that I received a standing ovation and the look on my opponents faces when I left the podium with the Governors still cheering, told me that neither one of them were prepared to follow that act.

As soon as I exited the conference building, I was mobbed by the press shouting their question. So I stopped and said, "Please forgive me, I don't have the time to answer your questions right now, but I will be releasing a detailed plan of my proposal to the press way before your deadlines gang, so don't panic. I'm sure once my Citizens Care proposal has been completely scrutinized; everyone will see it is just as viable as my other proposals. However, I would like to take this opportunity to mention that I will be hosting the ABC Powers television networks 2000, New Year's Eve Celebration this year, at the Disneyland Theme Park in

Forbidden Child III Exposed

Orlando, Florida.   I extend an invitation to all of America to celebrate the turn of the millennium with my family and me, along with many of our closest friends. For those of you who will be able to attend our celebration in person, I promise it will be the most extraordinary blow out New Year's Eve bash this world has ever seen.   Not only that, but the Disney Corporation, Universal Studios, and Sea World will be opening their parks for free that entire day, and Powers Inc. will be supplying all the amenities.   So if it's at all possible, please try to join us."

The next day the headlines read, **"Christina Powers takes a 68% lead in the polls after revealing her Citizens Care Program!   And since her invitation to the nation to join her in ushering in the New Millennium, there has been a record one hundred thousand reservations being made every hour at hotels throughout the State of Florida."**

Once again I dominated the headlines as the experts began their debating, but three days before Christmas I was knocked from the front pages again. Only this time it wasn't by any of my presidential opponents, it was by Mohammed. With captions like this one, **"King Mohammed stormed out of the peace talks in Moscow today and stated, 'President Puton is a stubborn arrogant man who is impossible to reason with.   This concerns me, as it should concern all, that such a man is seated at the helm of the second most powerful nation on earth.'**

Two days after these headlines I received a call from President Puton who said, "Christina, I have done all I can to stall the peace talks, but he is now threatening to begin an oil embargo if I continue to be so obstinate. With us heading into the worst winter ever predicted, and our banking system about to go broke I'm forced as

194

you Americans might say, to play hardball, because as you know we are still not capable of supplying all our own oil needs. To place my nation's people under such a hardship at this time could ultimately destroy the thin fabrics of our struggling democracy. But, I want you to know that I'm still in your corner."

"Please Nicolai, don't give in to him. I will help meet your nation's oil demand by giving you a cut rate from my Model Oil supplies."

"That's not a good idea Christina. If we do that then he will know for sure we are working together. Not only that, but he is promising to advance us three billion dollars to help stabilize our banking system before it collapses. I have no choice but to take the funds from him just to stabilize our fragile economy and try to keep our fledgling democracy on track."

I could hear the stress in his voice, so with a tone of confidence, I answered reassuringly, "I understand completely Nicolai, so please don't feel bad. Besides, I think you may have bought us enough time to beat him to the punch, and I promise, I will be in touch as soon as I'm in office. As for your banking cash flow problem I will transfer three hundred billion to your banking system tomorrow."

After that call Michael, Taylor, Jimmy, Pierre and I headed for Ravena to celebrate Christmas with Tess and the rest of Michael's family. It turned out to be the most heartwarming, loving, family, Christmas, I can remember. Not only were we rejoicing in the enthusiasm of my candidacy, but we were also celebrating the personal triumph of Michael's baby sister, Michelle, who had just received her Doctoral Degree in Psychology, as well as his niece, Mary's, wedding. Their excitement helped to make our Christmas even brighter that year. But like most cherished, peaceful, family gatherings, it ended too soon, and the morning after Christmas we found ourselves psyched to the hilt, as we all headed off to Orlando to prepare for our New Year's Eve celebration.

CHAPTER 26

As soon as we checked into our room that evening, Michael turned on the TV to catch the evening news. And we were stunned by what we were seeing, and hearing, as Dan Rather said, "Folks, we are witnessing the most phenomenal mass movement of humanity in American history. As an estimated two million Americans descend on the Orlando area. Just take a look at this footage, of the traffic jam on Interstate 95, with autos backed up from Florida to Virginia, and it's the same scene on all the major arterioles into the State. The traffic is so thick that officials at Powers Inc. are already parking vehicles in South Carolina, Georgia, and Alabama, and bussing their passengers into Orlando. Not only are the roadways backed up, but the airlines and railways are all struggling to meet the demand! But even with all the frustrations of the massive delays, it's apparent the spirits of those trying to get to Orlando are courteous, patient, friendly, and excited. This just goes to show us that when Christina Powers throws a party, she does it as she's lived her life, with flare. Now I'm going to step out of character for the first time in my career, to say I believe the woman is an absolute genius. And with the new figures giving her an astonishing 78% lead in the polls, it's clear to the world, it would take a miracle for anyone to beat her now."

By the time New Year's Eve morning arrived

**

there was an unprecedented two and a half million people filling the Orlando theme parks. We started the party 10:00 am on the nose. That morning was so sunny and breathtakingly beautiful, that the whole nation felt as if God were smiling on us. To make sure everyone was at the heart of the action Lucille, Barbara and Gloria had one hundred foot tall-screens strategically placed throughout the parks and in every major city across the country. The first thing I did that morning was introduce Barbara, to begin our celebration with the singing of the National Anthem.

Throughout the day I made cameo appearances and when the 9:00pm hour hit, I stayed on the stage and introduced one performance after another, as I enthusiastically built the excitement of the moment right up till forty minutes before midnight.

That's when I said, "Ladies and gentleman I'm going to leave the stage for a few moments and when I return I will be doing a number as a tribute to my mother Marilyn Monrow."

The audience cheered as I walked off the stage and when I returned I had on a blonde wig and was wearing an exact replica of the outfit my mother wore when she performed 'Diamonds Are A Girl's Best Friend'. I looked so much like my mother that the crowd went wild and when I started to perform the same routine as my mother did in 'Gentleman Prefer Blondes' the cheers were so loud we had to max out the volume on the sound system just to be heard.

When I finished my performance that night there was no doubt to anyone whose daughter I truly was. I was so proud of my true parents that I was beaming when I left the stage.

After a moving performance by Michael Wilson of 'My Way', I walked out on the stage and shouted,

"Way to go, America!" With that the audience let out with a roar. While they roared, I shouted again, "We sure know how to party, don't we?" And we cheered some more.

When we stopped cheering, I said, "My friends, I thank you for coming to celebrate this glorious day in history with us. Thanks to you, my heart has been filled to capacity with feelings of unconditional love, as we've all experienced the power of humanity united this day. That power has touched me so profoundly, that I am confident we will survive whatever the future may hold. Now on a more personal note, I would like to say that after 11:59pm this evening, I will be retiring from the entertainment industry to dedicate my life whether I win or lose this election, to saving the future for our children. That is why, while we're standing together ten minutes to the edge of a millennium; I would like to perform for you one last song which I've written just for this occasion."

With that they cheered and with tears of love and joy filling my eyes, I waved my arms in the air and the orchestra began. When I joined the orchestra, my voice echoed the lyrics with more power then I'd ever sung before,

"We are united at the dawn of a new millennium, with dreams so free, as we stand together to make history. For in your eyes I see visions, of what the world will be, when we take each hand and make our stand, to fight against the evils besieging this generation of man. For united is the only way we can defeat the darkness devouring our land and destroying the future, for our little ones.

If you would only hold my hand, and take that stand, then together we'll see the power of the spirit that burns within every woman, child, and man, as

Forbidden Child III Exposed

we conquer the darkness raging war all through our land.

So come walk with me, victoriously, into a future filled with endless impossibilities. `Cause I know when we've joined each hand, we'll have reached a power beyond the comprehension of man. Then together we will save the future, for our little ones. Oh for our little ones, we must join each hand, for our little ones, we must make that stand, for our little ones, we must save our land. And we will have done it, all, for our little ones.

Yes, for the little ones, whose spark of life flares in their eyes, with pure love so unconditional. So let's give them all, half the chance, to reach beyond the stars, and grasp their dreams, by fighting back the darkness, which is devouring, our air, land and sea. And we will have done it all, for our little ones.

For united we'll stand and together woman, child, and man, will conquer the darkness, devouring our land. So take my hand and we'll run carefree, like a child running to a playful sea, toward a future that will be, bright clean, and free. And we will have done it all, for our little ones. Oh for our little ones, we must join each hand, for our little ones, we must make that stand, for our little ones, we must save our land. And we will have done it all, for our little ones.

Oh for our little ones, we will join each hand, for our little ones, we will make that stand, for our little ones, we will save our land. And we will have done it all, for our little ones. And we will have done it, all, for our little ones', forever to be freeeeeee.

When the orchestra stopped the audience cheered so loud, I knew in my heart we were truly going to save

Forbidden Child III Exposed

our nation. Then I shouted, "I love you, America! God bless you all, and happy millennium!" With that the fire crackers filled the air and our cheers filled with love, pride, and hope, echoed across the country. Our celebration as one nation under God that night, was so spiritually moving, that we could feel the spirits of the angels rejoicing amongst us. For there were no Catholics, Protestants, Jews, Evangelicals, Muslims, Buddhist, Hindus, nor Blacks, Hispanics, Gays, Lesbians, Transgenders or Whites, there were only children of God, equal in body and soul. Nor was there an evil or judgmental remark heard, as we reveled in our oneness. And we took that feeling of oneness home with us in our hearts and onto the campaign trail when the celebrating ended.

CHAPTER 27

By the time we reached the Democratic Primary on July 27th, I had an 82% lead in the polls, but after they officially nominated Vice-President Sam Kal and Senator Ann Brown as their President and Vice-Presidential Candidates, my lead slipped to 60%.

Then on August 16th, after the Republicans officially nominated General Norman Howal, and New Jersey Governor Sheri Burns, for their President and Vice-Presidential Candidates, my lead slipped again, only this time it was to a reachable 48%. When we held the Independent Party's primary on August 24th, I knew I had to regain a strong lead and fast, because with Mohammed still lurking in the shadows, I didn't want there to be even a slim chance of possibly not winning this race. That's why I took the gamble and had Michael and our beloved eight year old son Taylor, stand with me when I addressed the assembly at the opening ceremonies.

I'll never forget that night when Michael and I stood beside our little man back stage, with only two minutes to go before I was to address the entire nation by opening the Independent Party's 2000, Primary Caucus. Taylor was so beautiful in his little blue tux, and his baby blue eyes just gleamed as he waited full of enthusiasm to help me with my address. I felt so proud of him as I knelt down and ruffled his silky dusty-blonde hair gently through my fingers.   I looked at him lovingly, and with a slight hint of nervousness in my voice said, "How are you feeling, honey?"

Michael interrupted with an enthusiastic, "He's going to do just fine, Mom."

With that Taylor smiled and confidently replied, "I'm all right, Mom. Just like Dad said, 'I'm going to do just fine,' so don't worry.   Besides Mom, don't you remember the lady in my dream?   She told me, Dad and me, were going to help you win, remember?"

I kissed his cheek and softly answered, "I remember, baby."

Just then Jimmy came running up to us and said, "They're ready!"   Then looking at Taylor he added, "Are you ready, little buddy?"

He answered with a smile, "I'm ready, Uncle Jimmy."   Then hugging Michael and me he continued, "I love you guys, don't worry."

"We love you too, son." Michael proudly answered.

I hugged him again and with tears in my eyes said, "I love you with all my heart, honey."   At that I grabbed Michael's hand, then looking at them both I added, "I'm so proud of you both, now let's go 'break a leg' guys." And off we went.

I proudly stood with my family at the podium and boisterously said, "Ladies and gentlemen of this delegation, my family and me, on behalf of the Independent Party's Chief Executives, welcome you to the Independent Party Year 2000 Primary Caucus."

After their cheers, I continued, "I have asked to open this caucus with my family, because we believe the futures of our children rides on the outcome of this Presidential race.   And as parents, my husband and I fear that if my proposals are not implemented in this nation and soon, we will not have a future for our children. We also know in our hearts as we look at our own son that if I'm given the chance, I will take the proper steps toward saving our environment. We will have a future with plenty of trees left to give us the fresh air we'll need to breathe in that future, because we'll be recycling everything. And we'll have clean water again, without all the acid, and disease causing bacteria, because we will stop our factories from polluting them. Also someday our streets and parks will be clean and safe for our children again, because our schools will replace the streets and malls for hangouts. It's as simple as that. Then not too far in the near future, everyone will truly begin to care for our planet again. And we'll have done it for our children. Now we ask you as a family, to join us by giving me your support." Then I looked at Michael and said, "What do you say, honey?"

He smiled and answered, "You've got my vote."

Then I lifted Taylor up and said, "How about you, little man?"

He smiled confidently as he answered, "On behalf of children all over the world, I cast our vote for my Mom 'Christina Powers' for President of the United States of America!"

Then we all waived as I said, "Thank you, and God Bless!" With that we received a standing ovation.

The next evening I won the Party's Nomination for President hands down. Immediately after the announcement, the national anthem began to play and everyone stood up. Afterwards the balloons fell as the cheers rang out. This went on for ten minutes and when things calmed down I said, "God bless you, America! And thanks to you, my vice-presidential candidate, the former President of the League of Women Voters,

Forbidden Child III Exposed

Barbara Goldstein and I, will be heading for the White House in November." And as they cheered I shouted, "But we're not going alone. Oh no, we're going five hundred and thirty five strong, and were not coming back until we've taken back the Congress!" With that their cheers turned into screams. Then, I shouted even louder, "Look out Washington, America's cleaning house!" And that's when they really lost it.

After the primaries we regained 9% of our losses, so heading into the debates we held a 57% lead in the polls. After much dickering with my opponents over the topics, we finally agreed on September 18th, to hold two debates. The first was to be held on October 12th, at California State University's Berkeley campus in San Francisco. The topics agreed upon were, Foreign Affairs, Crime, and National Defense. The second debate was to be held on November 2nd, at New York State University's New Paltz Campus in New Paltz, New York. The topics there would be Health Care, and The Nations deficits. Once the debates were finalized, I began studying between each campaign stop, every angle of the topics like a chess player. I had to make sure I knew every step either of my opponents might take, and be ready to respond accordingly. So when we reached the first debate on October 12th,, I felt more than ready to handle whatever surprises my opponents might present.

When I entered the auditorium at Berkeley the night of the first debate, I was cheered by the filled to capacity crowd. As I climbed the steps to the podium I waved to the press who were set up to beam our images all over the world, for what was built up by them, to be the most dramatic debates in America Political History.

Once I reached the podium, I greeted my opponents with a hardy hand shake, and some small talk as we waited the ten minutes until air time. The debate was being narrated by Dan Rather, Tom Holt, and Barbara Waters. By the luck of the draw, I was to be last of the three candidates to address the issues. This gave me the advantage, because I could then compare my issues to my opponents, while the public had them fresh in their minds.

As we chatted, the loud speaker came on, and Barbara Waters said, "May we please have everyone take their seats. We'll be beginning in just a moment now." With that I took my seat and thought, "Please, Lord help me make this good."

"Good evening America," Dan Rather began. "Welcome to Debates 2000! This is the first of two scheduled debates to be held between the three American Presidential Candidates. My colleagues, Barbara Waters, Tom Holt, and I will be narrating this evening. Now to begin the debates we go straight to our audience for the first question from a Mr. Tom Volpie."

With that Tom, who was standing at the mike set up in front of the auditorium said, "My question is on Foreign Affairs. Right now we are spending billions we can't afford, on maintaining the NATO alliance and the United Nations. And at a time when peace treaties are being signed all over the world, I have to wonder, why we don't take some of that money, and put it toward paying off our deficit instead of adding to it. Thank you."

With that Barbara Waters said, "The question goes to, Vice-President Sam Kal."

Sam cleared his voice and replied, "What I propose to do is to slash the four hundred billion we now spend on these programs in half, and add two hundred billion a year to paying off our deficit. Thank you."

Then Barbara said, "General Howal, the question

now goes to you."

The General shook his head slightly sarcastically, "We cannot cut these programs as the vice-president has suggested, but we can freeze the expenditures at current levels, and refuse all new applicants' entrance into NATO, as well as the U.N.. Thank you."

Barbara spoke up again, "The question now goes to, Ms. Powers."

I smiled warmly and replied, "I respectfully disagree with both my opponents' views. First if we are to learn anything from history, it should be that whenever people thought we were about to achieve world peace, a world war would break out. So that is why I would propose taking two hundred billion from our one trillion four hundred billion dollar holding fund, and invite the former Russian Block Nations, plus the current Russian Republic, into NATO. And because they have proven to the world that they believe in liberty and justice, we will grant them all, favored Nation Trading Status. Then we would strip China of that purchase right, and place 30% tariffs on all imports from China. We would continue to do this until they ban all the slave labor sweat shops and have proven to the world that there will never be another Tiananmen Square incident. China must allow freedom to flourish in the streets and in the hearts of their people once again. And the thirty billion we would earn on China's new tariffs will be channeled into helping the struggling economies of all the former Eastern Bloc Nations. Thank you."

This time Tom Holt began the narrating by saying, "Thank you Mr. Volpie, for your question. Our next question comes from, Mrs. Rose Shavone."

Rose wore a shy, warm, smile as she leaned into the mike to say, "Recently our nation's leaders have stated that the downsizing of our military has cut costs and increased productivity. My question is, if that were true then why do the statistics show there has been a 30% drop in the morale of our armed forces, because they feel they are being forced to work with unsafe and aging equipment thanks to Congress' new budget cuts. Thank you."

Then Tom said, "Mr. Vice-President, the question goes to you again sir."

Sam stood tall as he answered, "I agree there is a morale problem in our military today, and I agree that our military should be compensated appropriately for their loyal service to our nation. I also feel there is a need to upgrade our aging weapon systems. That is why I propose adding another one hundred billion dollars to our military budget. And since I won't have a fictitious holding fund to draw it from, I will eliminate the joint American-Russian Space Training Program, and funnel that one hundred billion into upgrading our Military and increasing their base salaries. Thank you"

Tom began again, "General Howal, the question goes to you now sir."

With a tone of disbelief the General said, "Mr. Vice-President, I'd rather stick my hand into the ladies' fictitious holding fund, and come up with nothing, before I'd cancel the Russian, American Space Program. Especially since all we need to do is pull one hundred billion from our three hundred billion dollar NATO budget."

With indignation Sam snapped back, "Being a General Sir, I would think you would prefer to have that one hundred billion in NATO, instead of outer space."

That's when Tom tried to say, "The rebuttals come at the end of the program, Gentlemen."

At the same time the General was angrily saying,

Forbidden Child III Exposed

"How dare you question my strategic abilities!"

That's when Dan jumped in, "Gentlemen, gentlemen, please. The question now goes to, Ms. Powers."

I smiled almost to the point of laughter then said, "Ladies and gentlemen of America, if my programs are implemented the military will have already received their largest salary increase ever, so morale would already be on its way up. And to keep bringing up morale, I would pull from our then existing holding fund, two hundred billion dollars and begin to update our weapon systems. I believe the most important thing for our nation's safety and security is to have a military no one in the world will want to challenge and if elected that will be my first priority. This is the only way to boost our military's morale and at the same time we will be boosting American Industry. Then we would eliminate the ridiculous, 'Don't ask, Don't tell Policy' of our current Administration, and allow all homosexuals the right to enter the military. Not only that, but we will allow homosexual couples the right to legally marry. These couples will be recognized, and honored in our nation as any heterosexual marriage is today. We will open up the doors for those couples who want to adopt children and allow them to do so. I know in my heart these couples will lovingly and eagerly adopt those children which have been abandoned to, and lost in, our current Child Welfare Programs. This will not only provide loving families for our forgotten children, but it will also save our nation millions of dollars in child care cost. Thank you."

With that Dan said, "Thank you Rose, for your question. Our next question comes from, Mrs. Violet Orland."

Violet wore a strong, proud, expression as she

stood at the mike and said, "My question is more of a concern to the American Family personally, because the crime in our cities is so out of control, it's to the point we're afraid to walk the streets in our own neighborhoods. And I for one want to know what you plan to do to help save our cities form this ever growing threat of violence?"

Dan began, "The question is once again on you, Mr. Vice-President."

Sam smiled confidently as he replied, "First, I would toughen the penalties for all crimes committed across the board, no matter what the crime. Second I would add five billion dollars to our nation's current crackdown on drug smuggling. Thank you."·

Then Dan said, "General, the question is yours sir."

The General's smile was even brighter then Sam's when he said, "This is something we agree upon Mr. Vice President, only your proposals are too weak to do any good. That's why I will make all drug offenses fall under federal guidelines, and enforce the death penalty in all fifty states for anyone caught dealing drugs to our nation's children. Thank you."

Dan cleared his voice and smiled as he said, "The question goes to you, Ms. Powers."

I smiled appropriately and answered, "Ladies and gentlemen, 80% of our nations crime today is drug related. So the answer to our problem would be to simply eliminate drug trafficking in our cities. This is clear to all the experts, and that is what our nation has been trying, and failing, to do for years now. Only we're finding that the way we're going about it is doing nothing more than merely scratching the surface of our drug trafficking problem, and sending us deeper in debt, as the drug cartels laugh all the way to their Swiss Bank

Accounts. Now that it's clear our strategies are not working, I think it's time to change strategy and beat the drug cartels at their own game. First, we would legalize all illegal drug use in this country and place it's usage under strict government controls. Second, we would produce the drug supply ourselves and drop the price right out from under the cartels' feet. Third, we would pass strict prison sentences on anyone caught with drugs in their possession, if they are not listed with the government as a user, or if the drug found on the person was not sold by the government. Fourth, we would offer to buy our drug supply from the cartels, thus making them a legitimate tax paying business, only it would be at a much lower price then they're getting now. And fifth, we would take the fifty billion dollars a year we would earn on the drug sales, and the fifty billion dollars we would save on our drug war with the cartels, and funnel that one hundred billion into our not so fictitious holding fund. Which by the way; will be holding one trillion one hundred billion dollars. The other thing we would do to help curb crime is to legalize all forms of prostitution because we are never going to be able to stop this behavior. We would do his by creating safe houses for prostitution where we would be able to test all the prostitutes and their 'johns'; thus, helping to prevent the spread of STD's. By doing this we would be offering a safe work environment for those who choose this career and put a stop to the abuse many of those in the field receive from their pimps. This could potentially save us fifty million dollars a year on court costs, fifty million a year on related medical expenses and bring another one hundred million dollars into our holding fund. Thank you."

With that the room gasped. Barbara quickly turned to face the audience, as she said, "Please, no outbursts." Then turning back toward the podium she continued, "The first rebuttal is on you, Mr. Vice President."

Sam looked straight at me and said, "You have some way out proposals' lady, but tonight's takes the cake. Legalizing drugs, prostitution and homosexual marriages in America is unheard of, and the American people would never stand for it. Thank you."

Barbara's face was nearly white as she said, "The next rebuttal is yours, General,"

The Generals dark cheeks were bright red as he said, "I agree completely with the Vice-President, only I think for Ms. Powers to even suggest legalizing drugs, prostitution and homosexual marriages in our nation, shows citizens she may not be such a former drug user after all. Not only that, but I think she should be barred from the next debate because of it. Thank you."

The whole audience looked like ghosts as Barbara, choking on her words said, "And the last rebuttal is yours, Ms. Powers."

I stood tall, calm, and cool as I replied, "I respect my opponents' opinions, but I strongly disagree with them. And I'm sure once America has had the opportunity to examine my drug reform package in detail everyone will see this is the only way we can truly fight and win the war on drugs, and drug related crimes in our nation. Not to mention the millions of lives and dollars, we will be saving from eliminating drug and prostitution related illnesses, like AIDS, STD's and Hepatitis. And as far as my proposal to allow homosexuals to marry, all I can say is, it is way past time we treat all our citizens equally. Thank you, America."

Barbara took a deep breath as she stared dead into the cameras and calmly said, "Well you heard it, America! And I'm sure we'll be hearing a lot more of it in the days to come.   Now on behalf of my colleagues and I we thank the candidates, and the American people, for making this debate possible."   And the moment she said, "Good night."   The room exploded into shouts of controversy.

As we were being ushered back stage by security I thought, "God, please help them see I'm right."

The next day the nation rocked and the headlines echoed the rumble for the next two weeks, with front pages like this one, **"Christina Powers shocks the world once again as she reveals her controversial Drug Reform, Foreign Affairs and National Defense Polices. At the same time her opponents remind the nation of her family ties to the mob, and her formerly known life style of drug abuse, sexual perversion and abortion. And as the accusations fly the numbers show Christina Powers is taking a beating because of it, with a whopping 15% nose dive in the polls."**

The next day's headlines were even better, **"China and the Arab world condemn Christina Powers' Foreign Polices as all of Eastern Europe applauds them, but still Christina slips another 5% in the polls."**

After that came the **big bang** as the headlines read, **"All the analysts agree Presidential Candidate 'Powers' Drug Reform Package could feasibly work. But she still loses another 5% of her lead in the polls."** And that brought these headlines, **"Undercover sources reveal, Drug Cartels have placed Christina Powers on the top of their hit list, to prevent her war on their drug industry. Even with this news Christina's lead still slips another 5%. As the polls slip we must ask, is Christina Powers really as in touch with the American People as we once thought she was?"** Even with all the controversy my programs and past lifestyle seemed to cause, I still managed to hold on to a 27% lead in the polls as we headed into the second debate.

CHAPTER 28

It was 7:46pm, November 2nd, when I entered the auditorium of New York State University's New Paltz Campus, for the start of the second debate. I knew this was my last shot at bringing it home for the entire Independent Party. This, I had to have because without them America would end up with nothing more than another lame duck administration, and I sure as hell didn't want that. So as usual I was prepared for anything including a little mudslinging, but what transpired that night surprised even me.

It seemed to begin the moment Peter Jensen said, "Good Evening America, and welcome to round two, of debates 2000. Where I, and my colleagues Maria Schreibert, and David Toppal, will be narrating tonight's eagerly awaited debate, between our three Presidential Candidates."

With that the cameras zoomed to Maria who said, "Since Health Care and The Nations Deficits are the only two issues slated for tonight's debates, the format will allow for a rebuttal following each issue. One final note, by the draw of the straw tonight's lineup will be Vice President Sam Kal, Business Entrepreneur Christina Powers, and General Norman Howal. Now without further delay, let's go to our audience for the first question from, Ms. Mildred Mancusco."

Mildred wore a meek smile as she leaned into the

mike and nervously said, "Good Evening Candidates, I am a member of the Duchess County Association for Senior Citizens, but I speak for the concerns of young and old alike, because the rising cost of Health Care today has us all frightened. And our question is, what will you do if elected, to help control and slow down those costs? Thank you."

This time it was David Topal who narrated, "Thank you, Mildred. Now the question goes to you, Mr. Vice-President."

Sam appeared very sure of himself as he began, "I plan to implement a National Health Care lottery, and the proceeds will go into our current State Medicaid Programs. Then we will begin to supply Health Care coverage to the twenty nine million Americans who have no insurance now.   And if we make this move today, we will begin to substantially reduce Health Care costs in the future. Thank you."

Then David said, "Ms. Powers, the question now goes to you."

I smiled confidently as I replied, "Today our Nation spends a total of eight hundred billion dollars a year on Health Care costs, and we boast the best Health Care System in the world. That is for those who have Comprehensive Health Insurance. But for those who aren't fully covered or have no insurance at all, it's the worst. This is why we must provide Comprehensive Health Insurance to all our citizens, without crippling or even compromising the quality of our Health Care in the slightest way. To do that I propose we first take one hundred billion dollars from our one trillion one hundred billion dollar holding fund, and invest it in our current medical research programs. This must be our first step, because with all the new diseases projected to be heading our way in the next few years, we need to establish a strong front-line defense. Second we would assume all Health Care insurance payments being made today, by our nation's employees and employers. Third we would mandate all current Health Care Insurance Companies and Home Health Care Providers, to hold open registration for every American citizen. Then the government will pay the increased insurance premiums, so we can provide all Americans with comprehensive health, eye care and dental coverage, without having to overhaul the current system by cutting costs, or diminishing the quality our Health Care Providers offer. Now to free ourselves from the Health Care nightmare we're in, and guarantee we will continue to have the best Health Care system in the world, will cost our nation one trillion two hundred billion dollars a year. To pay for this, we would take the one trillion from our holding fund. The other two hundred billion will come from placing a 10% land tax, on the two trillion dollars' worth of the tax exempt real estate held in our nation today, by its religious organizations. By stripping them of all their current tax exemptions, we will insure that our holding fund remains solvent indefinitely. Thank you."

The audience gasped as Peter Jensen said, "I must remind the audience members to please refrain from any further outbursts. Now the question goes to you, General."

The General turned to me and sarcastically shouted, "What are you the Anti-Christ lady?"

Peter interrupted, "General, the rebuttals come after you've answered the question sir." As Norman was still saying, "First you want to legalize drugs and homosexual marriages, now you want to tax the churches? What are you going to do next, take our children's college funds from them, because you think they won't have to pay for their education anymore?"

Forbidden Child III Exposed

Peter tried a second time, "General, please! We must follow the format."

Then the General snapped at Peter, "I'm fully aware of the format Jensen, you don't have to remind me."

Peter came back quickly, "Then please abide by it General, and answer the question."

The General was visibly angered as he said, "Both my opponents have missed the mark completely on solving our Health Care problems. Especially since all we have to do is put a mandatory freeze on all medical costs until our economic growth matches that of the medical field. Thank you."

Maria, with wide eyes said, "The first rebuttal is yours, Mr. Vice-President."

Sam shook his head dishearteningly and replied, "America, first I have to wonder if the General thinks we're all stupid. His proposal would do nothing but cripple our Health Care system, and he should know that. As for Ms. Powers, who wants to tax our churches, as she legalizes drugs and condones homosexual marriages; well, all I can say to that is, read the laws of God written by Moses, Paul, and all the apostles in your Bibles and then judge her accordingly. Thank you, America."

Maria lifted her eyebrows at me as if to say, 'Answer that one smart ass…' as she said, "The rebuttal is now yours, Ms. Powers."

I shook my head and shrugged my shoulders as I simply answered, "America, my proposal is one which will provide the best Health Care in the world, to all of our citizens. I also believe in my heart that if Christ were here today, he would require his churches to give all they had to the healing of the masses, not just 10%. And if everyone would just read the words of Christ in their Bibles, and stop reading the words of Moses, Paul, and all the apostles as the vice-president has suggested, then maybe we would all learn the true lessons of unconditional love.   After all, isn't that what Christ said God is, Love?   Thank you."

Maria looked startled, as she continued, "General, the rebuttal is yours sir."

Norman cleared his voice then sternly said, "Bravo Ms. Powers.   That truly was an excellent performance; especially coming from a woman who deliberately seduced one of our nation's most prominent religious leaders just to destroy his ministry.   But if you think, by simply making a profound correlation between Christ's healing ministry and our Nation's health care problems will magically convince the American public to let you get away with taxing our churches, then you're nuttier then I thought.   And just in case you haven't noticed Christina, Christ isn't here, so I suggest we try solving our nation's problems without him.   And as for you Mr. Vice-President, well your lottery program for our Nation's health care, isn't any better then what this woman has proposed.   Thank you."

I nearly bit my tongue and I struggled to keep my composure as David Topal said, "Thank you candidates, for those candid views.   Now we go back to our audience for the second question from, Mr. Edward Severino."

Edward wore a proud expression as he leaned into the mike to say, "Thank you Mr. Topal, and my question is how will your Administration combat our Nation's growing deficit?   Thank you."

David smiled as he said, "Thank you Edward, and once again the question first goes to you. Mr. Vice-President."

Sam glanced toward me as if to see if I were

listening, then said, "As I've said, I will have two hundred billion transferred from our U.N. and NATO expenses, into a fund to pay off our deficit. Then thanks to our health care lottery, we will be able to transfer another three hundred billion now spent on our Medicare, and Medicaid Programs, into this fund, thus giving us five hundred billion dollars extra a year to pay off our deficit. Thank you."

This time Peter began the narrating, "The question is now yours, Ms. Powers."

I rubbed my hands together and prayed to myself, 'God, please help me.' as I said, "Ladies and gentlemen, this is the Biggie. Because if we don't pay off are growing two trillion dollar deficit and soon, our Nation will be plunged into the darkest depression our people have ever known. If that happens, I know we won't survive it as a Democratic Nation. This is why I propose we create a Deficit Buster Superfund, and we will raise the revenue for this fund in four ways. First, we would take the current five cent soda bottle deposit many states have today, and make it national. Second, we would place an additional five cent surcharge on every glass, plastic, and aluminum container sold in our Nation. Third, we would place a one dollar surcharge on every hotel room, airline, bus, and train ticket, as well as every restaurant bill totaling over five dollars sold in our Nation. Fourth, we would place a ten cent surcharge on every dollar gambled in our Nation. By adding another one thousand dollars a year to a family's personal expenses for this fund, along with what we earn from our tourist industry, and American corporations, we will raise a phenomenal, nine trillion dollars a year. I promise you right now, this one step, will enable us to be a-debt-free Nation in only eight years. And once that is accomplished, we will eliminate all other superfund surcharges, along with all Federal taxes, except those on our churches, and we would still have a nine trillion dollar a year budge. America, I know the first eight years will be tough, but if you will do this with me, then at the end of those eight years we will have the wealthiest and most powerful Nation this world has ever known. Then, and only then; will we be able to help the rest of the world join us in saving our planet for our children. Thank you."

With that, the entire audience began to cheer as Peter said, "Please! No outbursts! It's not fair to the other Candidates." Once they calmed down, Peter continued, "Now please control yourselves from any further outbursts, thank you. The question now goes to you, General."

I could see on the General's face, he was past angry as he looked at me and said, "People, how can you let yourself be taken in by this woman? Just take a look at the life she's led, and you will see for yourself, she has no moral right to hold office as the President of our great Nation."

Peter interrupted by saying, "Please General, I've told you the rebuttals come after the answers."

The General shook his head with frustration as he continued, "I simply propose we institute a National budget buster lottery, and pay off our Nations deficit with the earnings. Thank you."

This time Maria began by saying, "The first rebuttal goes to you, Mr. Vice-President."

Sam stood defiant as he said, "America, I agree with the General. This woman is a known Hollywood harlot, and it would be a disgrace to our Nation if she were to become our next President. That reason alone should be enough for anyone not to vote for her. Thank you, America."

Forbidden Child III Exposed

Maria looked as though she was holding her breath when she said, "Ms. Powers, you have the next rebuttal."

I nodded my head politely, then said, "I wish the problems of Health Care, and our National deficit could be solved as simply as my opponents would like us to believe, but that is not reality. What is reality is the fact that it will take proposals like mine to get us out of the mess our current policies have created, and everyone here knows it. To do anything less, would only be providing the patient with a bandage when he needs major surgery. This is why I ask all of America right now for your vote for my candidacy, and everyone who is running with me on the Independent Party ballot. Or all we'll end up with is another do nothing administration. As for the remarks my opponents have made over my morals, you have been asked to read your bibles and if that's the case then I'd like to quote our Lord when He said, 'He who is here without sin, be the first to cast a stone' and the minute I said, "Thank you America, and God bless." Someone yelled, "Way to go, Christina!" And that's when the entire audience let out with a cheer, which took Maria, Peter, and David, two minutes to quiet down.

Once the room was calm Peter said, "General, the rebuttal is now yours."

The General looked at me, then to the audience, and with a disgusted tone said, "What kind of rebuttal can I come back with after a statement like that? So all I'm going to say is please give me your support on November 4th, Election Day 2000. Thank you America and May God be with us all."

With that Peter said, "Well America, we've reached the end of debates 2000. And now that you've heard the candidates address the issues, it's up to you to decide who will be going to the White House only two days from now by casting your votes. On behalf of myself and my colleagues, I'd like to thank the candidates and you the American people for making this debate possible. Good night, America."

That's when the audience resumed their cheering, and as they cheered, I went over to shake the hands of both my opponents. While I mingled with the other candidates, security came out on stage to usher us to our individual interviews with one of the debate narrators.

My interview was with Peter Jensen, and when I entered the press booth, Peter handed me a clip on mike as he instructed me where to sit. When I was settled, he said, "We'll be ready on three." Then holding his hand in the air, he lifted one finger at a time as he said, "One, two, and three. Good evening once again, America. Thank you for tuning into tonight's after the debates' candid interview with Presidential Candidate, Business Entrepreneur, Christina Powers." Then he turned to me and continued, "Thank you for joining us, Christina."

I smiled graciously as I replied, "Thank you for inviting me, Peter."

After which he continued by saying, "Christina, according to tonight's audience poll, you've won this evenings debate triumphantly. So my first question has got to be, after the intensity of tonight's debate, how does that news make you feel at this moment?"

This time my smile was one of relief as I answered, "I feel greatly encouraged Peter, because without the confidence and support of the American people, none of our dreams for a brighter future will be possible."

Peter smiled as if he were truly pleased for me as he asked his next question, "Christina, economy experts and government leaders all over the world are saying, you seem to have magically devised numerous innovative solutions for all our nations' problems today. It's comments like that, which make American citizens, want to know how you came up with your programs."

I chuckled slightly then said, "It was easy for me Peter, because all I did was analyze our Nation's problems, as if they were problems confronting any business.   Then I examined all the possible solutions for each problem and picked the best one solution.   It was as simple as that."

Peter Shook his head in amazement as he continued, "So what's next, Christina?"

I sighed wearily then said, "Well, for right now, I'd like to just spend tomorrow relaxing at home with my family.   Then on Election Day, Michael and I will be placing our votes at our local firehouse, and then heading for our campaign headquarters at Rockefeller Plaza in Manhattan, to await the election results with our family and friends."

Then Peter said, "Christina, are there any last words you'd like to say to our audience, before we sign off tonight?"

I was quick with the response to that one, as I said, "Only this, Peter.   America, when you place your votes two days from now, please remember if you truly want to change our Nation, then I must have your vote all across the Independent Party ballots.   Now I look forward to seeing you all at the polls on Election Day. Thank you and once again I'll say, May God Bless us all."

As soon as the interview ended, I walked out of the press booth to be tackled by Barbara, Jimmy, Taylor, and Michael, all screaming, "We did it!   We did it!"

CHAPTER 29

After the debate Jimmy and Pierre, took Taylor home to bed, as Michael, Barbara, Frank, Tom and I, headed to the Poughkeepsie Radisson, for our end of the campaign trail celebration party. At the party I gave a quick pep talk, after which I thanked everyone for a job well done. Then I said, "Now please go have a wonderful time my friends, because the Party is on me!" After about an hour, Michael and I said our goodbyes, and headed home.

We didn't arrive home until after 2:00am. After checking on Taylor, who was sleeping soundly, Michael and I cleaned up quickly and headed for bed ourselves. Once in bed together, Michael pulled me lovingly into his arms and gently said, "You did it, Punkie! And just think, in two days they'll be calling you, Madam President."

I kissed his chest as he spoke those words, then said, "I didn't do it honey, we all did." I lifted myself onto my elbows, so I could gaze into his eyes as I continued, "And I especially couldn't have done it without you, my love. You held me up when I was tired, and you encouraged me when I was down. You have been my strength and you and Taylor have been my inspiration through this whole long ordeal." I kissed him lovingly, and with tears in my eyes added, "I love you Michael, and I thank you for all of it. But most of all, I thank you for loving me."   With that he pulled me to him where we touched our oneness, as we melted into the fire of our loving passions.

The next morning November 3rd, Jimmy and Taylor woke us at 8:30am, by throwing a pile of newspapers on the bed.   When we sat up, Jimmy handed us both a cup of coffee, then plopped his ass on the bed beside me and said, "Wake up girlfriend, and take a look at these headlines."

With that I sipped my coffee and as I did, Taylor jumped between Michael and me, causing our coffees to spill as he excitedly said, "Listen to what the New York Post ran, guys, **'The polls give Christina Powers, and the entire Independent Party, a whopping 56% lead after her triumphant victory in last night's debates!'"**

When he finished, I kissed his cheek and said, "You've been hanging around your Uncle too much."

He returned my kiss and said, "Did you hear me, Mom?   I said you have a 56% lead in the polls!"

With that I jumped on him and began tickling him as I said, "Yes, I heard you honey, and it's wonderful news!   Now you take Uncle Jimmy and get out of here, so your father and I can get out of bed."

It wasn't fifteen minutes later, we were all downstairs having a peaceful family breakfast, when Carman entered the dining room with the phone in her hand and said, "Excuse me Christina, but its Pierre, he said it's urgent."

I thanked her as I took the phone and asked, "What is it, Pierre?"

His voice was panic stricken was he shouted, "Christina!   The President has granted a request from King Fehd, to withdraw two hundred billion dollars from the American Banking System!   And the bottom of the

Forbidden Child III Exposed

Stock Market is beginning to drop out as the banks head to Wall Street scrambling to raise the cash."

I was stunned for a moment then I said, "I don't understand. Why are the banks going to the stock market for the cash?"

Pierre's reply was a bit calmer, "Because that stupid President of ours, had Greenspine put a freeze on the Federal Reserve leaving the banks no option, but to go to the market."

With that news I became infuriated and it echoed in my quick response, "What! Is he nuts? Something like this could cripple Wall Street and he knows it."

Pierre's voice became anxious again as he yelled back, "What should I do?"

I thought for a moment then said, "Call President Metal of Switzerland, and tell him what's going on. Then tell him I need him to wire two hundred billion dollars from my Swiss Account, the number is 6627659826, to our Bank of New York Account. Just make sure it goes straight to our Manhattan Branch, and not through the Federal Reserve. Then start calling all our stock holders and tell them not to panic, because I'm on top of it. You got that?"

He nervously answered, "I got it, Christina."

Then I added, "Just keep your cool Pierre, and I'll be there in two minutes."

When I hung up the phone, Michael yelled, "Two hundred billion dollars! What the hell's going on?"

I yelled back, "Just come with me to the office, and I'll tell you on the way."

With that the four of us flew out of our chairs, as Michael yelled, "Can't we even get out of our PJ's?"

I hollered back, "There's no time!"

Then Jimmy yelled, "But it's pouring out!"

I turned to him and said, "You won't melt."

Then I shouted, "Carman, have James bring us a change of clothing." With that the four of us ran out the door, straight into a cold November downpour.

When we dashed into the command center of Powers Incorporated, Pierre had everyone on the phones to our stock holders, desperately trying to prevent them from panic selling. When I reached Pierre's side, he was on the phone with President Metal. I took the phone from him and swiftly said, "Jeff, its Christina. Do you know what's happening here?"

His voice was noticeably shaken as he answered, "I heard Christina, but I can't authorize that kind of withdrawal all at once."

My voice was sharp and to the point, "Jeff, President Baxter has got to be conspiring with Mohammed, to have authorized this withdrawal. And you know damn well, if Mohammed gets away with devastating the American economy, Switzerland will be next."

He grunted painfully then said, "I don't know, Christina. You're asking me to risk Mohammed's financial wrath, and you're not even in position as the President to run that interference you promised."

My voice echoed the urgency as I quickly replied, "Jeff, you know how he's been jockeying into position to devour our economies. He's just jumped the gun because he knows I'll stop him once I'm President. And, Jeff, if we don't jump the gun with him, we're not going to have a chance of stopping him; because he'll have crippled the American economy before I've even been sworn into office."

He grunted again then said, "All right, Christina. I'll start the transfer right now. I just hope you can handle him once he finds out."

With a sigh of relief I said, "Thank you Jeff, and

Forbidden Child III Exposed

don't worry about Mohammed. He's not in a good enough position to try and take this any further right now."

With that I hung up the phone and right on the spot, I started to change my clothes as fast and inconspicuously as I could. Then I called Martin Flynn, the President of the American Stock exchange and said, "Marty, its Christina Powers. I want you to inform the floor, I'll be covering the withdrawal in ten minutes, with a two hundred billion dollar deposit."

When I was finished with Marty, I turned to Ann Markel my assistant vice-president and said, "Ann, turn on the big screen TV. I want to see what's happening with the stocks exchange."

When the TV was turned on, we caught Dan Rather in mid-sentence excitedly saying, "And as Greenspine, the head of the Federal Reserve continues to deny the banks access to over one hundred billion dollars cash, the Dow Jones has just dropped another 60 points. America this is looking more like a 'Black Friday' than a pre-election Monday as the American banking system struggles to raise the cash for King Mohammed's two hundred billion dollar withdrawal."

Then he put his hand to his ear monitor as he began to shake his head with disbelief, and said, "Hold on, folks! We've just received word that Christina Powers has transferred two hundred billion dollars cash, from a Swiss Account into the Manhattan branch of the Bank of New York. And as the news of Christina Powers' incredible bailout of the American banking system hits the floor of the stock exchange, people are beginning to cheer as the stocks began the fastest rebound Wall Street has ever seen. This is unbelievable! Christina Powers has just prevented a Wall Street nightmare with one hell of a swift response."

With that announcement everyone in the room including myself began to cheer. And as we cheered I noticed that Dan went to correspondent Ken Carpenter in Washington. I couldn't hear what he was saying, but when the camera came back to Dan, he looked as if he had just seen a ghost, so I yelled out, "Everybody be quiet, something is up."

When we could hear again, Dan was saying, "We are witnessing an unprecedented turn of events America, as the United States Congress grants King Mohammed Fhed of Saudi Arabia, an on the spot approval to begin a two hundred billion dollar takeover attempt of Powers Incorporated."

With that news my blood begin to boil as I yelled, "Why those bastards! They're trying to destroy us." Then I turned to everyone in the room and started shouting orders, "Ann, get everybody on the lines to our foreign accounts, and start transferring our cash holdings to our American Accounts, now! And for God sakes, tell them not to let one-penny go through the Federal Reserve. Pierre, get President Metal back on the line! Michael, get the President on the line! Jimmy, you get Marty Flynn back on the line!"

Jimmy handed me the phone first, and with an angry tone I said, "Marty, begin a two hundred and twenty five billion counter offer for me, and stay on the line. We're going to fight that bastard until he takes cover in the oil muck he crawled out of!"

With that Pierre reached a phone out to me and said, "It's, President Metal."

I grabbed it quickly and forcefully said, "Jeff, I need that other one hundred billion dollars, and I need it now!"

All I heard was, "Aa! Aa!"

So I yelled, "Jeff, did you hear me?"

Forbidden Child III Exposed

Finally he nervously replied, "I heard you Christina, but I can't do it."

I snapped back, "What do you mean, you can't do it?   Don't you know what's going on here?"

I could hear the stress in his voice as he snapped back his reply, "Yes, dammit!   I know what's happening, but I can't help you now!   Mohammed just pulled five hundred billion cash out of our reserves!"

That punch nearly took my breath away as I shouted, "And you let him?"

He shouted back, "I had no choice; he was going to cut off our oil supply immediately if I didn't."

I sighed in anguish as I said, "You just slit our throats, Jeff."   With disgust in my voice I added, "I have to go."   And I hung up.

My heart began to pound so hard I thought my head was going to burst.   Then I buried my face into my hands, and when I looked up, all I could see were the frightened faces of those I loved counting on me.   So I took a deep breath and shouted, "Damn, him!   We're not licked yet, guys.   Pierre, get Al Greenspine from the Federal Reserve on the line pronto!   Michael, where's the damn President?"

Michael shouted, "I'm on hold!"

I shouted, "Ann, get Tom Davies on the phone. Tell him to publicly declare this takeover attempt illegal, and appeal to Congress to overturn its approval."

And as Ann screamed, "Gotcha!" Jimmy stuck a phone in my face and shouted, "It's Flynn, he needs you, now!"

I grabbed the phone and said, "What's happening, Marty?"

His voice was nearly quivering as he answered, "Mohammed just upped the ante to three hundred billion!"

Forbidden Child III Exposed

With force I answered, "Then counter the bastard by twenty five billion, and keep countering him until he retreats. And Marty, I want you to stay on the phone with Jimmy, and keep me informed." Then I handed the phone back to Jimmy as I shouted, "Ann, turn up that volume, I want to hear what Dan is saying."

The moment the volume was up we heard Dan Shouting, "Ladies and gentlemen, Wall Street is rallying once again as Christina Powers makes a two hundred and twenty five billion dollar counter offer in an attempt to block King Mohammed's takeover bid of Powers Incorporated. Hold on, America! It appears as though the battle is on: as we receive word that in the last ten minutes the offer and counter offers taking place between these two financial giants for ownership of Powers Inc., has reached four hundred billion dollars and climbing. As this battle wages on Wall Street, sources at Powers Inc. tell us all attempts by Christina Powers to reach the President, to try and convince him to block this foreign takeover attempt of Powers Inc. have been simply placed on hold."

With that Michael grabbed my shoulder as he said, "It's the, President."

I took the phone and calmly said, "Bill, I implore you to put a stop to this battle by declaring this takeover attempt illegal, thus null and void."

He arrogantly replied, "I'm not stopping anything, Ms. Powers! America is a free market Nation, and this type of corporate battle is what makes our free market so profitable. Don't you remember?"

I answered with a dignified tone, "I remember quite well Mr. President, but this is a hostile foreign invader, who is trying to take ownership of what amounts to nearly one third of our Nation's largest corporations. And that adds up to economic treason

Mr. President, and you know it!"

He raised his voice angrily as he answered, "Christina, this is a world market we live in today and there's no such thing as national loyalty anymore. So I'm afraid you're on your own." And as he said, "Now I must go, I don't want to keep my caddy waiting."

I was shouting, "Up yours' you bastard!" And I slammed the phone down so hard, it broke in half.

That's when Jimmy shouted, "Christina! We've reached five hundred and twenty five billion!"

Hearing that I turned quickly toward Ann and asked, "What do we have in foreign currency?"

She nervously snapped back the answer, "Seven hundred billion, Christina."

Then Pierre anxiously shouted, "Christina, its Al Greenspine." as he tossed me a cordless phone.

I snatched it in one hand and demandingly said, "Al, I have nine hundred billion dollars on deposit in American banks, and you're illegally keeping it from me knowing that Powers Inc. is under a congressionally sanctioned hostile foreign corporate takeover attempt. Now I expect you to abide by the law, and release those funds for me right now, so I can at least have a fighting chance of winning this battle."

With all that he calmly asked, "And if I refuse?"

So I calmly answered, "I'll hang you by you balls for treason, the moment I take office."

He calmly replied, "Consider it done."

So I simply said, "Thank you." As I hung up the phone, I threw my fist into the air and shouted, "Yes!" And once I did, everyone began cheering again.

When everyone stopped cheering we became fixed to the TV screen to hear Dan saying, "As soon as the word hit Wall Street, Al Greenspine released the hold on the Federal Reserve allowing Christina Powers access to nine hundred billion dollars Powers Inc. has on deposit, King Mohammed raised his takeover attempt to a phenomenal one trillion dollars, causing the stocks of Powers Inc. to soar to unheard of heights. As Wall Street waits for a counter offer from Christina, the panic selling that's taking place on the floor has sent the stock markets across the board plummeting into a spiraling nose dive. Now the question everyone is asking, is, 'Will the American economy survive what's being called, the battle of the giants?'"

I turned to Frank and shouted, "Frank get President Puton on the line for me now!"

As soon as President Puton was on the line I said, "Nicolai, I know you know what's happening here and I need you to transfer the three hundred billion I deposited into your Nation's banks into my account now and I'll get it back to you as soon as this is over."

He calmly replied, "I can't do that Christina."

"What do you mean you can't do that, if I lose Powers Inc. we will all be at his mercy."

He started to laugh at me sadistically then said, "Well now you know how the big boys play you stupid bitch!"

I could almost feel flames shooting out from my eyes as I shouted, "You prick! No one double crosses me and gets away with it! I'll be coming after you next you bastard!" Then I threw the phone across the room and it shattered all over the floor.

With that my heart lodged in my throat and as I swallowed it, Jimmy stuck a phone in my face and said, "It's, Flynn!"

I took the phone to hear Marty screaming, "Christina! It's one trillion dollars, what the fuck do you want me to do?"

My mouth was so dry, I was coughing on my

words as I answered, "Counter Marty, and keep countering. That is until we've reached another six hundred billion. If that happens, get back on the line with Jimmy, and I'll tell you what to do next."

When I handed the phone back to Jimmy, he grabbed my hand and with a look of desperation said, "That's everything we have, Christina!   All of it!"

I squeezed his hand reassuringly and answered, "I know Jimmy, but we can't let him win."

From out of the blue, Pierre said, "No it's not!"

I turned toward him and said, "What do you mean?"

He smiled as he answered, "There is still six hundred billion in our employee pension accounts."

With that, Ann said, "We can't touch that, it's illegal."

I looked at her and asked, "Who is heading our union negotiation team?"

She answered quickly, "Joe Aiello."

I smiled and said, "Great! Get him on the line for me." Then I turned to everyone in the room and shouted, "Get on the phones right now, guys. I want every employee we have to stop working and start watching Dan's report.   I want them to see for themselves the battle we're in, before I ask them to commit their pension to the fight."   Turning to Michael I added, "Get a phone link to every business we have, and then have them get ready to patch me in on their intercom systems. I need to address every employee personally."

Just then I gazed over quickly to see Taylor nervously fidgeting with some papers, as he sat in the swivel captain's chair, three feet from me, at the head of the command center. When he caught my glance, he smiled warmly, and then motioned his lips to silently say, "I love you, Mom."

I immediately placed my arm around his shoulders, as I knelt at his side to whisper in his ear, "I love you too, Punkie Doodle. Are you doing all right?"

He slanted his head toward me and gazing deep in my eyes said, "I'm scared, Mom."

Squeezing him tightly, I confidently said, "Don't you worry, baby, we're going to get through this just fine."

As I held my baby reassuringly, I heard Ann saying, "Excuse me Christina, but I have Joe on the line."

I kissed Taylor's cheek and said, "Say a little prayer for us, okay." I kissed him again and continued, "I love you, baby, but I have to go back to work now. Just remember Daddy and I, are right here if you need us."

He smiled as he nodded his head and said, "All right, Mom."

When I stood up, I thanked Ann then asked, "Did you brief him on our situation?" She nodded a 'yes', so when I took the phone I simply said, "Joe, I need you to set up a tell-a-link with the heads of all our unions for me, and I need it in ten minutes. Now I'm giving you back to Ann, and I want you guys to keep this line open." Then I added, "Are you going to be able to handle this for me, Joe?"

With a tone of unequivocal confidence he answered, "I'll be talking with you in ten minutes, Christina."

I replied, "Great, Joe, I'll be waiting."

When I handed the phone back to Ann, Michael's secretary Lucille Karatzas came up to me and nervously said, "Christina, there has got to be a hundred thousand reporters surrounding the building, and they're all screaming for a comment from you."

I patted her shoulder reassuringly and said, "Tell them I'm busy."

Then Michael yelled, "Its ready, Christina. Our employees are watching Dan's report and the intercom system is set up so they can all hear you."

I turned to Ann and said, "Is Joe ready?" All she could do was nervously nod 'no.'

Just then, Taylor yelled out into the chaotic pace of the room, "Mom! They're flashing a red emergency bulletin across the screen."

All eyes and ears hit the TV to hear Dan say, "America, we've just learned that Congress has denied the petition made by attorneys from Powers Inc., to declare King Mohammed's takeover attempt of Powers Inc. illegal and order it null and void." Beginning to shake his head he added, "Hold on, folks! We are getting more. It seems events are catapulting out of control so rapidly in this volatile battle, we can hardly report it fast enough." Then he nodded his head to someone off to his left and said, "I got it!" Turning back to the camera he added; "It appears as the battle reaches the one trillion three hundred billion dollar mark, Christina Powers will be addressing the four hundred thousand American employees who work for Powers Inc. via a phone call which will be patched into their intercom systems. When she does, we will be airing it live."

That's when Ann said, "Christina, its Joe."

I calmly reached for the phone, cleared my voice and said, "Are you ready for me, Joe?"

He confidently replied, "Go ahead Christina, everyone can hear you."

I took a deep breath, swallowed hard and abruptly said, "Good Morning, this is Christina Powers,

President of Powers Incorporated and your employer. By now I'm sure you're all aware we have been battling a hostile foreign corporate takeover attempt of Powers Inc., by King Mohammed Fhed of Saudi Arabia. This battle has only been raging forty nine minutes, and we've already reached one trillion three hundred billion dollars. That figure can only tell us one thing. Mohammed wants to own nearly one third of America's industries, which breaks down to your jobs, as well as mine, and he wants it bad! But I promise you, as long as I have the ability to fight him, he won't get it. Now I don't know how long this battle will continue, but I do know if we lose it, Powers Inc. as it is known today, will be bankrupt, and Mohammed will have taken control of what will become the wealthiest and most powerful corporation on the face of the earth; because whoever wins takes the whole pot, which adds up to the money and the corporation. The reason I've brought this to your attention, is to ask you to join me in this battle to save our families' livelihoods, and keep ownership of Powers Inc. in American hands, by allowing me to use the six hundred billion dollars, which belongs to you, the employees of Powers Inc., in your pension plans, as a little insurance policy in our battle to block this hostile takeover attempt. I know what I am asking is a lot, but I hope you can see what's really at stake here. Now due to the urgency of the situation, I'm going to ask you all to decide for yourselves whether I may access those funds or not, by holding an on the spot vote. I need your answers as soon as possible. Thank you."

We turned back to the TV screen to hear Dan saying, "You heard it, America. This is a high stakes battle and with the stakes rising, Christina turns to her employees, for as she put it, 'a little insurance policy.' As of this minute the battle stands with Christina's

Forbidden Child III Exposed

counter offer of one trillion four hundred and twenty five billion dollars. Now we're going to switch over to Ken Carpenter in Washington where top Church leaders, along with thousands of citizens are gathering outside the White House demanding the President order a stop to this madness."

That's when Ann handed me a phone and said, "It's Joe Aiello."

I took another deep breath as I grabbed the phone and said, "What kind of news do you have for me, Joe?"

He shouted his answer, "You got it, unanimously!"

With tears welling in my eyes I shouted back, "God bless you, Joe."   Then I shouted to everyone in the room, "They're with us," which caused everyone to let out a cheer that sounded a lot like a sigh of relief.

When we stopped cheering, it was back to the TV and Dan, who was excitedly saying, "America, it's been nearly ten minutes and Wall Street has still not received a counter offer from King Fhed. And as far as we know, Christina has not had a reply from the employees of Powers Inc. either." His eyes lit up as he continued, "Hold on a minute folks, we've just learned that Marty Flynn, the President of the American Stock Exchange, is about to make a public announcement. Right now we're going live to Wall Street and our correspondent, Dorothy Diguida, 'Dorothy, can you give us a clue as to what Marty will be announcing?'"

The camera went to the stock exchange balcony and Dorothy, who said, "Dan, I'm sure he wants to calm the market as quickly as possible. I'm also sure he's hoping the fact that fifteen minutes have passed without a counter offer by King Fhed, will help him do just that."

Then Dan asked, "What's the mood on the floor Dorothy?"

Forbidden Child III Exposed

She simply said, "I can only describe it as panic Dan, take a look for yourself."   Then she waved her arm for the camera to span the floor, and as it did, the whole world got to see the havoc and fear this battle was creating on the faces of everyone in that room. As we watched, Dorothy interrupted, "Hold on Dan, Marty's about to address the floor now."

When the camera zoomed to Marty, he straightened his suit jacket and said, "Ladies and gentlemen, I have faxed three formal requests to King Fhed, asking for his counter offer and each one was declined. So it appears that at one trillion four hundred and twenty five billion dollars, Christina Powers saves the American economy from a devastating blow, as she wins her battle to keep controlling interest of Powers Inc., and remain President of its Board of Directors." With that the floor began to cheer. And when they cheered we all cheered.

When we finally calmed down enough to hear Dan again, he was saying, "It's not even noon yet America, and this has been the most incredible day in the history of the American Stock Exchange, as the woman the world is now calling, 'America's tiger' saves the day. As the news spreads across the country, the markets are already showing signs of a possible quick rebound."

That news lifted a ton of weight from my heart, and the moment I sighed with a sense of relief, Dan's voice took on an air of shock and urgency as he shouted, "Oh My, God! America, we've just learned the United Arab Emirate, China and Russia have joined King Mohammed, in his attempt to takeover Powers Inc., by upping the ante to a whopping two trillion dollars! And once again it appears the next move is up to Christina Powers. But with a ball this size being thrown into her court, the question now is, 'Will she be able to counter this one?'"

When I heard that I grabbed for the closest chair, as my legs nearly gave out from under me. Then I clutched my blouse and with my soul in anguish cried out, "Lord Jesus, Devine Mercy, help us! I don't know what else to do." And as if being struck by a bolt of lightning, it hit me. Then I shook my head in an attempt to slow my thoughts as I quickly turned to Michael and said, "Call a press conference on the front lawn immediately."

He looked at me with wondering eyes and replied, "It's still pouring out honey. I'll call it in the lobby."

I grabbed his hand forcefully and said, "It has to be outside."

He hugged me tenderly, "I'll go set it up right now." When he left the room, I began to pace the floor in deep thought.

Within five minutes Michael opened the door and said, "They're ready for you, baby."

I ran my fingers through my hair in an attempt to look like something, and as I did, Taylor ran to my side, grabbed my leg and began to cry. I snatched him up into my arms, held him tightly and fought back the tears as I gently said, "Oh baby, don't cry. No matter what happens we'll be all right, I promise you."

Michael flung his arms around us both and confidently said, "Hold on guys. I know we're going to win this."

I kissed them both, and as I handed Taylor to Michael, I caught sight of the teary eyed faces on everyone in the room, so I stood tall and defiantly said, "There's no way he's going to beat us." When I left that room, there was a speck of hope rekindled in every heart.

The moment I exited the front door of Powers

Inc., the sound of the cameras snapping startled me as it overpowered the pounding of the rain. I stopped for a split second to see thousands of people gathered in the cold downpour, breathlessly waiting my response and I thought, "God, please guide my words." Then I swallowed hard and began to walk across the parking lot toward the open field where the microphones for the press were deliberately set up in front of the towering pine forest which ran along the banks of the majestically beautiful Hudson River. By the time I reached the mikes and took my place in front of the cameras with this awesome display of Mother Nature behind me, I looked like a drowning rat. Then I pushed back the wet hair from my face, and with all the strength I could muster said, "America, I stand here to tell you this is not just a battle for Powers Incorporated any longer. It has become a battle for America's financial survival. The reason it has become that, is because it is a calculated conspiracy to commit financial treason against the American people by our own Government Leaders, because they know come tomorrow night they will all be ousted. They have sold us out for great gain I'm sure, to the oil rich Arab nations who are at this very minute attempting to devastate our economy, and financially enslave us. Mohammed is orchestrating all this because he knows with our current financial might, we will break the chains of oil that bind us, and his ability to one day financially rule the world will have been destroyed."

 With that the rain seemed to begin to fall harder, and I found myself flinging my arms out from me, so the drops could be seen bouncing from my flesh. Then I shook my arms forcefully for a moment before continuing, "People, do you see this rain? Can you feel it beating on your skin? Well I pray you can, because they're the tears of the Spirit of God being poured out for all life on this precious Mother Earth of ours.   The spirit is crying, because it knows this isn't just a battle between Mohammed and Powers Inc. for the survival of America; no, this is a battle between good and evil, for the survival of the human race.   And if we don't stand together right now to defeat this force of evil attracting our Nation, then this will become America's darkest hour, and our dreams for a brighter future will be ashes blowing in a toxic wind.   This is why I have fought, and will continue to fight this battle.   But the reason I stand in the pouring rain right now is to plead with corporate America to join me in this battle to save our Nation, because I know without you it cannot be won.   And if you think I may be mistaken concerning Mohammed's intentions, just take a look at your current stock levels, and you will realize once he obtains Powers Inc. he will be in a perfect position to swoop down and completely devour the entire American Stock Exchange, and at rock bottom prices.   Now with the blessing of my entire staff, I'm going back inside and I'm going to fight that bastard until I can fight no longer.   On my way back, I'm going to pray that you join me.   Thank you and May God be with us all."   With that everyone began to cheer, even press members, and as I headed back toward the building they followed me cheering all the way.   When I entered the building, everyone inside began to cheer.

Once I entered the command center, I took the phone from Jimmy and forcefully said, "Marty, counter offer, and don't stop until it reaches two trillion five hundred billion."   Then I handed the phone back to Jimmy, and walked over to where Michael and Taylor were standing.

We all just stood transfixed to the screen as Dan said, "What we just heard America, was a heart wrenching plea for the survival of our Nation.   Inside sources tell us that Christina Powers has just countered King Mohammed, with an offer of two trillion twenty five billion dollars. As we wait for the counter offer, all America sits breathless on the edge of our seats wondering, will 'Corporate America' respond to Christina's plea?" With that his eyes lit up as he grabbed his headset and began shouting, "Hold on! Hold on! You're going too fast." Then he screamed, "America, Wall Street is rocking again as the Disney Corp. commits five hundred billion dollars to the battle. Wait! Universal Studios just matched it. Listen to this folks; Exxon and Texaco have jointly committed eight hundred billion dollars." Then with tears beginning to flow from his eyes he shouted, "Christina, I know you're watching. Listen to this, American citizens by the thousands are offering to put up their life savings and their homes to join the fight. Hell, I'll give twenty million myself!" Then he wiped the tears from his cheek with his sleeve, and with a choked voice said, "God Bless You, Christina."

With that, we all began to jump up and down hugging one another as we wildly screamed, "We won! We won!" And when we finally calmed down enough to pay attention to Dan again, it was just in time to see him jump out of his seat and shout, "America, we've just learned that King Mohammed, China, Russia and the United Arab Emirate, have just backed down to the financial might of a united industrial America, by declaring they will cease all further attempts to obtain Powers Inc." And I'm sure you can imagine how we all reacted to that news.

It took us at least twenty minutes just to contain ourselves enough to head home. When I opened the front door to leave the building, I was shocked to see that the rainy morning had given way to a sun filled afternoon and there was the most beautiful double rainbow right over our heads that I had ever seen. Once the crowd saw me coming, they began to shout in loving unison, "Christina! Christina!"

I was so moved that I started to cry and as I wiped the tears from my cheeks I thought, "God, thank you for getting us this far."

The next night as I waited alone in my room at Rockefeller Center for the election results I heard a tap on the door, and the soft loving voice that followed was Michael's. "Christina, may I come in?"

I answered, "Come on in, the door is open, honey."

When he reached my side, I stood up to embrace him, and putting his arms around me he lovingly said, "Are you all right, Punkie?"

I kissed his cheek and replied, "I couldn't be better, Michael."

With that Taylor and Jimmy ran in the room together, and as Taylor excitedly said, "Mom, they're about to announce the winner!" Jimmy flipped on the TV to once again see Dan Rather, only this time he was saying,

"Ladies and gentlemen, it's not even 9:00pm, here in New York yet, and after the largest voter turnout in American history, we can safely say Christina Powers has won her bid for President of the United States of America with an unprecedented 97% of the popular vote, which gives her an across the board sweep of the electoral vote. Not only that, but she's taking the entire Independent Party to Washington with her."

We could hear the entire city come alive as they shouted victoriously. Then Dan shouted, "And this news has just brought the house down here at Rockefeller Center, and from the reports we're getting, it's the same scene all over the Nation as our citizens take to the streets.   As the country celebrates, we here at the Powers Campaign Headquarters will be waiting for Christina to come down and give her acceptance speech."

I clicked off the set and the minute I did, my personal phone, which was lying on the desk began to ring.   Michael's eyes opened wide as he looked at me and said, "Do you think?"

As I reached for the phone I replied, "I'm sure it is."   So I answered by calmly saying, "I'll bet you two trillion dollars you're not wearing that smirk on your face now, Mohammed."He screamed with hatred in his voice as he snapped back, "You, bitch!   You may have won this one Christina, but I've only begun to fight."

I replied with a condescending tone, "I've told you once Mohammed and I'm going to tell you again. You haven't seen anything yet.   Now I really must go collect the spoils of my victory by taking the helm of the most powerful Nation on earth."   I hung up the phone, grabbed Taylor's right hand, Michael's left and said, "Well first family, let's go greet our relatives."   With that we headed for the ball room.

When we walked out on the stage the cheers of love, and joy, which rang out, had the power to bring tears of pride to the eyes of every American no matter where in the world they were at that moment.   As we reached the podium I thought, "God, this is just the beginning.   I know we still have so many more hurdles to leap before we reach our goals."   I gazed back at the cheering crowd and thought, "There's still, Mohammed, 'Lord,' what will we do the next time he rears his evil fangs?"   With that I glanced at Taylor and Michael, who were both gleaming with pride and this time I thought, **"Oh well, I'll figure it out tomorrow…"**

James Aiello

Forbidden Child III Exposed

This novel is dedicated to America with love from your friend, James Aiello